RITA MURPHY

Published by
Dell Laurel-Leaf
an imprint of
Random House Children's Books
a division of Random House, Inc.
1540 Broadway
New York, New York 10036

ISBN 0-440-22837-9

RL: 4.6

Reprinted by arrangement with Delacorte Press

Printed in the United States of America

April 2002

10 9 8 7 6 5 4 3 2 1

For all the women who taught me to fly
And for Ed, Liam, and Dewey,
the men who believed

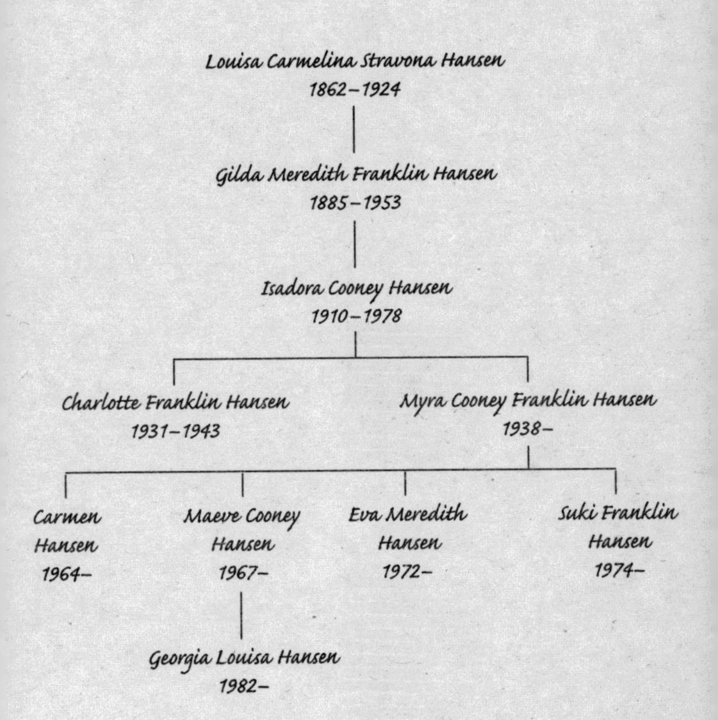
Louisa Carmelina Stravona Hansen
1862–1924
Gilda Meredith Franklin Hansen
1885–1953
Isadora Cooney Hansen
1910–1978
Charlotte Franklin Hansen
1931–1943
Myra Cooney Franklin Hansen
1938–
Carmen Hansen
1964–
Maeve Cooney Hansen
1967–
Eva Meredith Hansen
1972–
Suki Franklin Hansen
1974–
Georgia Louisa Hansen
1982–

Night Flying

Chapter 1

The Hansen women have always flown at night, even in bad weather. Aunt Eva actually prefers storms. She says she makes better time that way. Though often she ends up on the east end of town and has to walk back along the railroad bed if the wind isn't blowing in her favor.

Flying is something we do at night when everyone is asleep. Twice around the meadow or once over the ridge to clear our heads before settling in for the evening.

My aunt Suki stayed out all night once when she was sixteen. She went to the county line at Madison. She wanted to see how far she could go.

"That's the danger with young fliers," Mama says. "They don't know when to turn back." Suki was in bed for two days after with a fever and cramps.

It's not an easy thing to do. Flying. Not like you'd think. There are wind currents and air pockets, and birds. Don't ever underestimate birds. It can be difficult to see a swallow coming in at dusk. And even though owls have excellent night vision, there have been collisions, and they aren't pretty.

"It's best to stay close to home when you're starting," Mama says. "It's best not to take too many chances."

* * *

The first woman in our family to fly was Louisa Hansen, my great-great-great-grandmother. She came to America from Albania more than one hundred years ago. A dark, wiry woman full of Gypsy blood. They say it was her broken heart that propelled her to flight, her grief that sent her soaring out over the sea.

Louisa lost her husband and little boy in a shipwreck off the coast of Newfoundland in 1884. She survived along with seven others, rescued by a fishing schooner. She eventually married one of the fishermen aboard, Jonathan Hansen, and went to live with him in his house by the ocean. They say she started flying in her sleep out over the cliffs, searching for her lost loved ones, returning in the early hours of the morning drenched in sea spray.

Since that time, every Hansen woman has flown. Aunt Eva says it's like a family full of acrobats or mountain climbers. Once one generation believes they can fly, it makes it possible for the next to believe too. The only thing that's unique about our family is that we haven't forgotten. We still believe.

As far as I know, we are the only family of fliers in Hawthorne. There are perhaps hundreds, thousands of women in the world who fly, but it's hard to know who they are. You can never tell just by looking at someone. Most fliers lead rather ordinary lives.

Aunt Eva believes any woman can fly regardless of body shape or weight. It is only those who believe they can, who feel it with no doubt, who succeed. You can never let doubt creep in. Not even into the smallest corner of your mind, or you'll fall right out of the sky.

Like all the women in my family, I have been flying since the day I was born. My aunt Eva was the one chosen to take me up the first time. She is my godmother and the strongest flier. She has the arms of a swimmer. Arms that never give up. She's been known to fly for five or six hours without landing.

I know why Mama chose Eva to take me. She wanted me to feel Eva's confidence. When I was strapped to my aunt's chest, the feeling of flight went deep into my bones, and it has never gone away.

* * *

Three generations of Hansen women live in our house. We're out on the county road as far as you can go. It's a rambling old Victorian that belonged to my great-grandmother Isadora Cooney Hansen. She painted the entire house blue in 1928. Inside and out. It was her favorite color. The kitchen is teal blue and the third floor is sky meadow blue and the outside is periwinkle with navy trim. Over the years, my aunts have painted their own rooms rose and cream, and the pantry is no longer sea green but a mellow yellow. Everything else is still blue, though, including the insides of all the closets.

There are eight fireplaces and six bathrooms, four with claw-foot tubs so deep you can lose yourself in them, and one long, winding staircase reaching to the third floor. A ladder leads from the third-floor landing to the widow's walk on top of the house. I am the only person who goes up there anymore. Mama and my aunts used to smoke in the walk when they were my age, and there are still a few mementos left of their time there. A stack of old fashion magazines filled with pictures of skinny women in bell-bottom jeans and shag haircuts, a case of empty Coca-Cola bottles, a couple of ashtrays shaped like fish.

I go to the walk in the early morning when everyone is asleep except Mama, who gets up before dawn to cook or hang out laundry. My aunts stay up late flying, so they tend to sleep in. Often they don't come down for breakfast until noon. Grandmother never rises before ten.

I have two aunts who live with me. Suki and Eva.

Suki is the youngest. She has fair skin, blond hair, and blue eyes with horn-rimmed glasses. Suki plays the clarinet and piano and most any other instrument she can get her hands on. A consistent flier with superior navigational abilities, Suki can find true north without a compass in the fog.

Eva is two years older than Suki. She is a painter and wears bright silk scarves, which hang haphazardly from her tall frame. Her curly auburn hair is cut close to her head and always looks messy, as if she just woke up. She wears silver earrings that stretch halfway down her neck. Eva can talk about anything to anyone. She is my prime source of information about family history.

My mother, Maeve, is five years older than Eva. Petite and pretty in a delicate way. She never soloed and hasn't flown since the day I was born. Even though Eva says Mama was the best flier in the family once, Grandmother will no longer allow it. In our family, Grandmother makes all the rules. She can't have anyone around who is better at something or more powerful than she is. Motherhood empowers a flier, and Grandmother could never live in the same house with a daughter who was both a mother and a talented flier.

Grandmother is not someone you want to cross. Even though she had many lovers when she was young, you'd never know it now. Her face is taut and severe and she is built exactly like a house. She wears practical shoes with thick waffle soles and prefers the color gray to all others. There is something about Grandmother that reminds me of a piece of granite. Cold, dusty, dry. The kind of surface you wouldn't want to land on hard or come up against if it was moving fast in your direction.

I must look like my father—except for my eyes, which are like Mama's. I have long black hair and olive skin. I am tall and thin and extraordinarily flat-chested.

The only thing I know about my father is that he wandered down our road one spring evening looking for access to the river. He was a scientist from the University of Vermont, studying the migration of geese, and our property extends down to the wildlife reserve. His hair was as black as a raven's and his skin a deep olive. Mama was so young, only fifteen at the time. She was in love. She said my father reminded her of the night. Cool and dark.

He left the day after Mama met him and she never saw him again, which was convenient since Grandmother would never have permitted him to stay. She is clear about this with all of us. No men are allowed to live on the premises. Grandmother believes that if men found out about our flying, peace would be lost, the magic would be gone. They'd want us to fly in the daylight so they could keep an eye on us. I don't believe Mama or my aunts hold to this way of thinking, and neither do I. I actually think it would be nice to have some more men around once in a while for variety.

The history of the Hansen fliers is full of ridiculous rules like that. Grandmother says, "No men living on the premises." Great-grandmother Isadora said, "No meat." Great-great-grandmother Gilda said, "No flying in the daylight." Great-great-great-grandmother Louisa said we must keep Hansen as our last name. Maybe if I stay around long enough, I'll make up a rule of my own and it will be "No more rules."

No one in my family works in the traditional sense. Grandmother has taken care of that. Her father invented the clasp that connects the little red float in the toilet tank to the skinny metal arm that moves up and down. The Cooney Clasp generated a fortune, which Grandmother invested wisely. It is not used on modern toilets. But, of course, every toilet in our house still has one.

Grandmother had me study that little arm, float, and clasp once when I was six years old and had thrown a box of crayons down the toilet.

"Do you see this little arm here, Georgia?" She flicked it with her finger. I nodded.

"See how it will not move?"

I peered over the edge into the rusted tank, afraid of what I might see floating in there. But there were only water and the arm with a red rubber ball attached to the end of it.

"Well, we cannot have that. No, we cannot. Your

great-grandfather, Harold Esmit Cooney, devoted his life to making things easier for people. He designed this little clasp to move up and down." She pointed to a small rusted piece of metal at the elbow of the arm.

"Because of your little experiment today, it cannot move at all. Paralyzed." She stood looking down at me, hands on her wide hips, waiting for the impact of her words to seep into my six-year-old brain.

"I think the arm looks awfully tired, Grandmother. I think it needs a rest," I told her.

Grandmother was not to be led off course. "Georgia, you must free the arm. That is your mission this afternoon. I am leaving a plunger, scoop, and bucket." She pointed out each object, laid neatly on the floor by the tub.

"These are your tools. I do not care how long it takes you. You must free it. Good luck." She turned and walked out of the bathroom, closing the door behind her.

Mama and Suki told me later that night, after I had successfully freed the arm, that they had been given the same lecture when they were my age for throwing marbles and carrot sticks down the toilet.

"It's a rite of passage in this house, honey," Suki told me.

I did not understand what sort of passage she could mean. All I could imagine was a long, dark, narrow tunnel winding down from the toilet to a secret cavern beneath the house.

"The clasp has a special meaning for Grandmother," Mama offered in explanation. "For all of us, really. It's what allows us the freedom to fly, to pursue our individual . . ." She could not find the word. "Our individual . . . pursuits."

"We call it the toilet money," Suki said, and we all laughed.

⋆ ⋆ ⋆

In a house full of women, it is nice to have a place to escape to. A place away from the chatter. I am a listener. A watcher. I am most at home in the widow's walk, writing down my dreams in an old leather-bound journal I keep hidden beneath the sofa, and looking down on life at the Hansen estate. I am a scientist of sorts, like my father. I watch the comings and goings of the women in my family as if they were tiny ants on the floor of the rain forest. In and out. Up and down. Talking all the time.

In the mornings I climb the ladder, push open the hatch, pull myself up onto the bare wood floor of the walk. It is a round room with no walls, only windows. There are suncatchers hanging from each one, so when the light strikes, it sends strips of watery color across the old red velvet sofa and along the floorboards.

From up here, I can see south all the way to Garrison and down into the Hawthorne Valley. On clear days, the Redborn Mountain Fire Tower is visible to the east. The light at sunset reflects off the silver skeleton atop the rangers' station, making it look like a tall, skinny man holding his arms out to his sides as if to say, "I don't know, do you?"

To the north there is nothing but open meadow and hills down to the Missisquoi River. In the fall, the snow geese come to the river to rest on their way south. One day, usually near my birthday, they arrive. A formation of silver-white bodies like a troop of angels blanketing the sky above our house.

To the west is the ridge. It is a cliff that drops off fifty feet into a deep ravine. That is where we take off from. It is the best place to catch the wind. Takeoff is usually the hardest part for young fliers. It can be scary, if you think about it too much. It takes practice, but it isn't nearly as difficult for me as landing is.

Looking down at the ridge, I remember last night's practice flight with Eva. As always, it was dark when we went, so I couldn't see the edge. I had to feel with my bare feet where the grass gave way to sharp rock. Since I'm still in training, Eva ran with me and held my hand until I was ready to let go. "Run as fast as you can, honey, so you won't think," she told me. Enough air had to build up under my stomach and chest so that by the time I reached the edge I just lay into it real easy and it took me.

Once I caught the breeze, it was pretty much up to me. I knew I couldn't go higher than Eva, so I stayed within the boundaries she laid out. Eva is always right beside me, so I couldn't just fly away even if I wanted to, which I do sometimes. I have dreams of taking off into the night sky alone. Soaring up and over the treetops. No one watching me. No one telling me where I can go or what I can do. No rules to follow. I am as free as a hawk or a falcon. Flying up into the inky blackness where the air is thin and the stars seem within reach.

We wear black when we fly so if we're spotted we're only a shadow against the sky, like a very large bat. We can fly pretty high. Ten thousand feet before we get the giggles and maybe another two thousand before we have to start back. It's a myth that anyone could fly to the moon or near to the sun. No one would get close to going above oxygen level. Some have tried, but it's a sad thing when a flier goes too high, when she doesn't know her own limits. Sometimes she doesn't come back, or if she does she won't ever fly again.

I can imagine how it happens, though. How you could forget yourself when you're alone and fly higher and higher. There is no feeling in the world like giving in to the wind when it picks you up. It's like being lifted by a gentle hand. When you fly solo and start climbing there isn't anyone beside you telling you stop. It's just you and the ocean of air around you. The earth below is so small, so unimportant, there seems no reason to ever come down.

That's when you have to remember the words of your mother or aunt, whoever taught you. You have to remember your duty to keep the tradition alive. You have to follow the first rule of flying: Be home before dawn always and without exception.

The Hansen women are good at keeping a low profile. If we're blown off course by bad weather we come down in a quiet spot. No one knows about our flying, but they suspect us of other things. We are not witches, though that's what some folks say. We have no power to cast spells or work charms, except Aunt Carmen, whom I never met. Suki says Carmen is like a witch, but not as predictable.

Carmen is my third aunt, the eldest of my mother's sisters. She lives on the other side of the country, in a house by the ocean where the winds are strong. No one mentions Carmen except Mama, and she only talks about her at night when the others are in bed or out of the house flying. It's strange the way Mama speaks of her sister in hushed tones, as if she has died. Mama says that in Grandmother's eyes she has.

I don't know what Carmen did to be sent away forever. I imagine it must have been something horrible or maybe nothing much at all. Perhaps she was cast out of the family for painting her room the wrong color. Who knows? That's the hardest part about living under Grandmother's rules: not knowing when or if you'll be told to leave one day.

I've asked Mama many times to tell me what Carmen did, so I can make sure never to do it myself. But Mama only says, "Carmen didn't follow the rules, Georgia. She can't be trusted. She'll hurt herself one day. But at least since she's gone, she can no longer hurt us."

Chapter 2

Mama calls me down from the walk. It's Saturday and we always go to town to pick up groceries and the mail on Saturday. We take Beulah, our old Volvo station wagon, painted pale beige on one side and brown on the other. She is a Beulah in every way—a sweet-smelling Southern woman who hums a little when she walks and will always take care of you. We have been caught in a couple of bad snowstorms with Beulah and have not once doubted she would get us through. She doesn't have four-wheel drive or anything fancy like that. She just has weight and composure.

We park outside the post office and I walk over to Wally's Market. Mama has no patience for shopping, so the job always falls to me. The first thing I do is read the bulletin board. A long white board nailed to the front of Wally's store full of tack holes and splashed with mud, waterlogged from being out in too many long winters. There are notices for foliage festivals and chicken pie suppers, apartments for rent in Hawthorne, yoga classes. These do not interest me. I am looking for a horse. For four years I have been looking for one.

Even though our house is constantly buzzing with the presence of my aunts and Mama and Grandmother, sometimes in all that buzzing, I start feeling lost, like I don't belong. I'm the odd woman out most of the time. Too young to share their secrets, too old to be their baby. A horse would be something just for me.

I've been taking riding lessons ever since I was seven years old at Barkley Stables, three miles from our house. It isn't a fancy stable like the ones over in Garrison, but they have some good horses. For the past five years, I've been riding an old chestnut gelding named Mic, with a good disposition and not many teeth. I take him out on easy trails and spend most of my time rubbing him down and giving him oats. He's sweet, but I'm ready for my own horse.

Unfortunately, Grandmother does not like horses and says that a girl my age should be doing other things with her time. I have asked and pleaded and begged, but to no avail. Once Grandmother makes up her mind about something there is no changing it. Grandmother has never had any experience with animals. She doesn't understand what it's like to care for a horse or ride on its back. It's different from flying. When I'm riding I'm part of the horse. I love taking Mic out at sunset or in early spring when the trees are budding. I love the strength of his body beneath me and the feeling of freedom.

Even though Grandmother refuses to consider my requests, I haven't given up all hope. I still look at the board outside Wally's every Saturday and imagine. Today there are two goats and a llama for sale. *Maybe next week*, I think as I enter the store.

When I was a little girl I used to be afraid to go inside Wally's alone. The aisles are stacked to the ceiling with miscellaneous housewares and food items and not one shelf looks stable enough to hold the weight upon it. I always worried that one of those shelves would collapse and bury me beneath a mound of groceries and I'd be lost under there forever. Now I'm old enough to know that if a shelf does fall, someone will get me out. Eventually. Above me fans hang precariously from wires on the ceiling and everywhere there are the smells of hay and dog food and fish, though to my knowledge they do not sell fish at Wally's.

Everyone who works there is related in one way or another to Wally, who is now almost a hundred years old and living in a nursing home in Nebraska. It was the only place that would accept him—he's as ornery as they come. I met Wally once when I was eight years old. He was standing at the checkout arguing with a customer over the price of pork. He was a crooked little man with a thatch of white hair sprouting from his scalp like a cornstalk. He wore a pair of overalls two sizes too big over his long underwear. At the end of the argument he cleared his throat and spit over his shoulder onto the floor a few inches from my feet, glared at me, and walked away.

Wally's grandson, a shy man with a bushy gray beard, runs the store now, and I have never seen him spit. Wally's granddaughters operate all the cash registers. They are in their sixties. I've often thought it would be nice to work somewhere, get out from under the watchful eye of Grandmother for a few hours after school each day, but I've never thought of trying to get a job at Wally's. There are too many great-great-relatives waiting in the wings. The competition overwhelms me.

I walk directly to the deli in back and order half a pound of baked ham and a quarter pound of Swiss cheese plus two hard rolls. Everyone in my family is a vegetarian. The Hansens gave up meat when Great-grandmother Isadora came up with her diet for fliers. She believed meat weighed you down, cut your energy, and contributed to accidents. She suggested eating healthy, airy foods. Rice, beans, broccoli. Anything that grows above the ground. Root vegetables are tolerated but not encouraged.

My family thinks I am a vegetarian too, and I do

not tell them otherwise. They are too stubborn to argue with. I make two sandwiches right there in front of Mrs. Shroeder, who runs the deli and who is a distant cousin to Wally. She is a large, round woman with huge breasts and no waist to speak of. She smiles at me as I take my sandwiches to the picnic table out behind the store and eat them slowly.

I will be sixteen years old next Thursday and I have never had a date. Somehow I believe it is because I have eaten so little red meat in my life. How is it possible for a growing girl to develop breasts on a diet of tofu and beans? Aunt Eva describes me as tall and thin and wispy. "You are built exactly like a ballet dancer," she says with an envious sigh. But I don't want to be a ballet dancer. I want to be curvy so if a boy grabs me one day, he'll have something to hold on to. If I eat two ham sandwiches every Saturday for the rest of my life, maybe I will grow firm and buxom. My breasts will fill out all my sweaters and Eva will no longer sigh over my thin, wispy figure.

After I finish eating, I wipe the crumbs off my face and go back inside. I fill the cart with soy milk, veggie burgers, and seaweed. I pull pale tofu and tempeh off the refrigerated shelf, throw in a couple of packages of malt balls, and smile to myself. I pick Mrs. Gunther's checkout aisle because she doesn't talk much and rarely looks at me funny like the other women at the store. We Hansens are a mystery in Hawthorne because we keep to ourselves, and some people are uncomfortable with mystery. But Mrs. Gunther only asks how school is, to which I can safely reply, "Fine," and she is satisfied.

Actually school is not fine. It isn't terrible, but it isn't great either. It is difficult being the only flier in a class of earth-dwellers. Some mornings I am so tired from a night of flying I can barely keep my eyes open. Mrs. Wrigley, the school nurse, is concerned about me. I have been sent to her twice this month for falling asleep at my desk.

"You know, dear, girls your age need extra sleep. Are you getting enough?"

What I'd like to tell her is, "No, I'm not. I've been out all night practicing for my solo flight later this month, and I popped my right ear from the altitude." But of course I do not. I say, "Oh, don't worry about me, Mrs. Wrigley, I'll be just fine."

I bring the groceries back to Beulah, walk to the post office, and glance inside. No Mama. I look up Main Street to the cafe and back down to Wally's, but there is no sign of her. I turn toward the park and spot her blue sweater. She sits on a bench, her head barely clearing the top of it.

Mama is the smallest woman I know. Her wrists are so tiny I could circle them with my fingers when I was five years old. Grandmother says she has a delicate constitution because of the fever. Mama had rheumatic fever as a baby and it weakened her heart so she didn't grow so well. I sneak up behind her.

Her head is bent—she is reading. I tap her on the shoulder.

"Oh, Georgia!" She jumps. "You scared me, honey." Quickly she folds the letter she is reading into her purse.

"What is that? A love letter?" I ask.

She swats me with her hand. "No, of course not. How was shopping? Did you find everything?"

I pull a malt ball out of my pocket and pop it in my mouth. Nod. "Any good mail?" I ask, looking over her shoulder. "Anything for me?"

She hands me a coupon booklet from Johnson Hardware and a flyer for a new weight-loss program at the Unitarian church. "That's it?" I ask.

Mama smiles. "That's it. Why, were you expecting something in particular?"

"No, just hoping," I say. I know girls my age receive letters from boys, but that's not really what I want. I'm waiting for something to happen to me. Something to come through the U.S. mail that will change my life forever.

Mama stuffs a fat bundle of letters into her purse. "The rest is for your grandmother."

It is disgusting how much mail my grandmother receives every day. Letters from lawyers and bankers and real estate brokers. Urgent official packages and who knows what else. It is unjust that a young, potentially buxom young woman like myself gets flyers and coupons, and a sixty-year-old woman in the middle of Nowhere, Vermont, has enough letters to build a house with. I sigh.

"Maybe, next Saturday there will be something for you," Mama offers in consolation. But I know next Saturday there will be another fat bundle addressed to Myra Cooney Franklin Hansen, as there has always been.

On the way home, Mama is quiet. She lets me drive Beulah even though I don't have a learner's permit. She says any young woman who can fly of her own accord two thousand feet above the earth can operate a station wagon going thirty miles an hour, which is the speed I must maintain for Mama's peace of mind.

Saturday mornings are the only time Mama and I are alone together. Sometimes on the drive home, I get this odd sensation in my stomach. A lurching, hurried feeling like I know this is my one chance to really talk to Mama, get close to her, but I don't know how. Sometimes I'm not even sure if I want to. I think Mama feels it too, because she makes little comments about how much she enjoys this time, or wouldn't it be nice to go on a picnic together in the upper meadow like we used to when I was little.

Once she reached over and put her hand over my hand and I almost pulled it away. I can't explain it, really. I have this feeling that if I let myself get too close to her I'll suffocate. I'll be like her, and even though I love her, I never want to be like her.

What usually ends up happening is that we sit in silence or talk about small, unimportant things like what to have for dinner or hasn't this been a short leaf season. When we arrive home, Mama helps me put away the groceries, then disappears upstairs and closes her bedroom door.

* * *

Every Saturday night I eat dinner at my friend Alice's. Her house is within walking distance of mine. I have to pass a couple of broken-down trailers on my way to Alice's that belong to Seth Orkin and his brother, Armand. They are old-time Vermonters. They still consider Grandmother a flatlander even though she was born in our house and has lived every one of her sixty years in it. From Armand's perspective, you're not a true Vermonter unless you're third or fourth generation, like me. During mud season, Armand occasionally offers to push Beulah when she gets stuck, and Seth will give us a tip on where to find dry wood, but other than that, we don't see much of them. Their yard is littered with junk cars and plumbing equipment and they keep two ferocious German shepherds chained up out back. I walk by quickly.

Alice and her mother, Grace, on the other hand, live in a fairy house. It is made of wood and has a turret, wind chimes hung from doorways, and bells tied to trees in the front yard. Suki loves to fly over their house on a windy night. She says it sounds like an orchestra warming up in the forest.

Grace is a midwife. When Alice was little, she spent a lot of time at our house when Grace had late-night births. It seems like those are the only kind she's ever had. Alice goes with Grace now. She is extremely knowledgeable about the female anatomy. I've learned everything I know from the two of them. They are like walking encyclopedias but much more interesting.

When we were young, Alice and I used to play with Grace's pregnant dolls. Each doll had a different-size belly, depending upon which week it represented. Grace used these to show her ladies what to expect. Once we took Grace's hand-sewn uterus, a stuffed version of the real thing, to use as a house for our dolls. When Grace discovered that it was missing and we were the culprits, she carefully explained to us how it worked. How the baby fits inside and makes its way out what seemed like a very small opening. Then she returned it to the top of her bookshelf so we wouldn't spill orange juice on it. "Uteruses are expensive, girls. This one alone cost twenty-five dollars." Alice says the only thing that makes Grace angry is not being able to find her uterus when a client is coming over for the first time.

We never played with regular little girls' dolls like Barbie. Grace said those dolls make normal people feel bad, like Alice because she's not skinny. Alice is very pretty, although people don't always think so when they first meet her because of her weight. Alice says when you're not built like a Barbie doll, people can't see past your flesh. They see you coming and they think, *Fat girl*. She doesn't seem too troubled by it, though. All the women in her family are large. "It's the way God made me," Alice says.

At Alice's house, things are looser. I am free to speak as I like. When everyone else around you is talking about vulvas and vaginas, it makes it easier to express your feelings. I'm not sure why this is. Perhaps it's because they've already said the unmentionable. There is no subject off limits after that. There are no taboos here, no secrets to keep. Not like at my house.

The funny thing is if I told Alice and Grace that I occasionally fly over their house on a clear night, they wouldn't be surprised. Grace would probably say, "Why, Georgia, honey, I always knew you had hidden talents." Grace has seen most everything. She is not easily shocked. Of course, I can't tell them about the flying, though I wish I could. I wish there were just one person in the world I could be myself with.

Grace is half Abenaki and half Irish. She is tall and broad-shouldered with strong hands, which have caught hundreds of babies. The walls of her kitchen and office are plastered with photos of little black or bald heads above wrinkled red faces. There must be more than four hundred photographs by now.

Besides being a midwife, Grace is a great cook. She makes all kinds of exotic dishes with meat in them. At first I thought she made these especially for me once a week, but Alice told me she and Grace eat like this every night.

Tonight we are having Moroccan chicken and couscous, with brandied pears for dessert. Little fan-shaped carrots decorate the side of the plate. I wish Grandmother could taste how wonderful meat is and change her rules for once. But I'm glad I am the only one who is invited to come here.

After dinner, Grace gives me a book of dreams and a new journal as an early birthday present. Alice and Grace have been writing down their dreams for years. They are always giving me articles and books on the subject.

When I was nine years old, I had a recurring dream about a wild black horse that ran around me in circles. It had gold bells tied to its mane, and the faster it ran, the louder the bells rang. I would chase that wild horse until my legs were about to collapse, and just when I got close enough to grab its reins, it would burst into flames and there would be nothing left but a small pile of black ashes on the ground in front of me.

I don't know why, but I told Grace my dream and she was excited I had remembered so many details.

She had me write them all down on the back page of one of her seed catalogs and draw a picture of the horse, the flames, and the pile of ashes.

Grace thought my dream was important. She thinks all dreams are important. "Whenever you're confused or don't know what to do, Georgia," she tells me, "just ask for a dream before you go to sleep and pay attention to whatever comes." I've been keeping track of my dreams ever since. Grace gives me a new journal every six months to encourage me. I tuck the book and journal inside my backpack and we settle into the first of three games of Scrabble.

Alice wins every game, and then Grace gets a call from one of her ladies and I gather my things to leave. On the phone Grace is telling Katie Byron to breathe and relax and make sure her mother is coming to pick up the other children. "You don't need to be worrying about John's sore throat now," Grace tells her. "Just focus on this baby." She hangs up.

"It's her third," she explains to us. "So she might go fast." Grace collects her things.

We walk outside together. It is chilly, the smell of woodsmoke in the air, a few stars. Grace does not offer to drive me home because she knows I like to walk at night. She is convinced that, like her, I have native blood running through my veins. "I love to see a young woman unafraid of the natural world," she tells me. Maybe it's native blood or maybe it's just that I've been out in the night since I was a baby, but

I love to walk home alone on Saturdays. I don't mind not seeing everything right away. If you give it a little time, your night vision takes over and things come into focus on their own.

I take the path at the end of Grace's driveway that leads through the woods to the upper meadow of our property. The Hansen family cemetery is up there. An acre plot surrounded by dogwood trees, five gray stones sticking up from the ground like crooked teeth.

Remembering the dead is an old family tradition going back to the first Hansen fliers. When Great-grandmother Isadora bought this property in 1928, the first thing she did was set aside a piece of land for the family cemetery. She wanted to have all her ancestors nearby, surround herself with the legacy of their flying so she'd never forget the tradition as she passed it down to her own daughters.

Isadora had stones engraved for her mother and grandmother, though Louisa's and Gilda's bodies aren't here. Louisa asked to be buried at sea, and Gilda was lost on a flight over Labrador in 1953, so her bones could be anywhere. I never met my great-grandmother, but Mama and my aunts knew her well. They've told me stories about what a hard, stubborn woman she was. Mama sleeps in her old room on the second floor. There is a portrait of her hanging over the bureau. A tiny, stern-looking woman with fire-red hair. I don't know if Isadora buried anything under Louisa's or Gilda's stone. If she did, I hope it was something substantial like a tooth or a lock of hair. Something that would draw them here. I like to think that their spirits pass by on clear nights like this, dipping low enough over the pines to catch a glimpse of me.

Next to Louisa's and Gilda's stones stands one for Charlotte Franklin Hansen, Grandmother's older sister. Grandmother never speaks of her, and if it weren't for the stone bearing her name, I would never have known she existed. Eva told me the story a couple of years ago. Isadora told her.

Charlotte was Great-grandfather Harold's favorite child. He'd take her fishing down at the river or into town to buy licorice whips. Isadora said they spent every day together. One winter morning Harold and Charlotte went skating and when they came home, Harold was angry. Isadora speculated that Charlotte had met a boy at the rink and Harold was jealous. But no one knew for sure. He sent Charlotte to her room and started drinking, and when Harold drank he was loud and mean. He'd never been angry with Charlotte before and it frightened her. She snuck out of her room at dusk; the weather was changing. She ran off the cliff to get away from him. Flew alone out into a late-winter storm and never came back. She was twelve years old. Isadora wrapped up Grandmother, who was only five at the time, and left the house. Left all the lights on and the stove burning.

She brought Grandmother to a neighbor's and went out in search of her eldest daughter. She flew all night long but never found her.

Eva thinks Isadora buried Charlotte's baby hair beneath the stone. A bright red curl, but for some reason Isadora would never say. Engraved on Charlotte's stone are the words "For the one who flew too high. Dear Lord Have Mercy."

Next to Charlotte lies Isadora, and then several feet away, set off on its own, stands Harold's stone. They are the only ones really here. I suppose Grandmother and Mama and my aunts will be buried up here one day. There's plenty of room. Maybe I will be too.

Though Grandmother follows all other family traditions, this one she does not keep. She never comes here. The cemetery would be overgrown with weeds if I didn't visit once in a while and pull the tallest ones away from the stones. In summer I pick daisies for each grave. This time of year I clear away leaves. I am not afraid of cemeteries. At least not old Vermont plots like this with few actual bodies in them. Sometimes when Eva won't go flying and Mama and Suki are busy I come up here and hang out with my other relatives. They are good listeners.

When I reach the house, the only lights on are one in Mama's room and Grandmother's reading lamp. Everyone eats an early dinner on Saturday and then goes off to their own pursuits.

As I walk past Mama's bedroom, I hear the voices of my aunts. They are all in there together. This is not unusual. My aunts often end up in Mama's room, strewn across the bed or camped out in sleeping bags on the floor. It is like a never-ending slumber party for them. I'm invited sometimes, but mostly I just let them do their sister thing without me.

I can tell from Mama's tone of voice that whatever they are discussing in there tonight is not normal slumber-party chat. It sounds serious. I would stay up and try to hear what it's all about, but I'm tired, and besides, all my aunts have the unfortunate quality of never being able to keep a secret for more than twenty-four hours. It will come out, I am sure, before sunset tomorrow.

Sometimes I find it strange, all these unmarried women under one roof. I wonder why my aunts never left to make lives of their own. Or why Mama didn't just run away with my father when she had the chance. I guess it's just too much work to leave the only place you've ever known. Especially when you carry a secret as big as our family's flying.

And there's the toilet money. It must be hard to give that up. Because that's what you'd be doing if you left. Toilet money only applies to permanent residents of the Hansen estate. Once you've left, even if you come back later, you have forfeited your claim. The rules are clear on that. I don't think I'll be able to stay, constrained by someone else's rules. I've already figured out what I'm going to do when I'm ready to leave. I'll invent my own gizmo. How hard can it be, anyway? I'll come up with an idea for floating underwear or edible pencils kids can chew on in school and not get lead poisoning. Something totally impractical that will drive Grandmother crazy. I'll make millions and free us all from the bondage of the family legacy.

Chapter 3

Sunday morning I wake later than usual because of the wind. All night it blew. Squirt, my black cat, kept dashing around my room, jumping at the shadows of tree branches on the wall. Wind makes her crazy. I must have had ten dreams, most of them filled with flying objects and people who could not speak. They only hummed and whistled and I couldn't understand anything they were trying to tell me.

Every hour or so I was awakened by the barn door banging open and closed. I guess no one else slept very well either, because when I arrive in the kitchen it is empty and there are three overturned coffee cups in the drainer. A sure sign Mama and my aunts were up most of the night talking.

The clock above the stove says eleven. I glance up

the stairs to the landing. Grandmother's door is closed. On Sunday mornings, Eva makes waffles and hot chocolate. Rice waffles and roasted carob and soy milk, actually, but still, it feels special. It is the only meal of the week we all eat together. Since Mama is given Sunday mornings off from cooking, it can be close to noon before Eva cracks an egg or squeezes an orange for juice. I'm so hungry this morning, I can't wait. I will come down later and have a second breakfast when they're all here.

I pour a bowl of granola and pop two slices of spelt bread in the toaster. Put water on for tea. I have a strong craving for bacon this morning, but that is a hopeless dream. No pork has come near one of these skillets since Great-grandmother passed down her diet for fliers.

I take my meager breakfast upstairs balanced on my book of dreams, grab Squirt under my arm, and head for the widow's walk. First I toss up Squirt; then I slide my book carefully over my head onto the floor above without spilling a drop of tea. Finally I pull myself up. I set everything out on the table next to the sofa. A window is open a crack and it is chilly. I go over to close it and notice Mama and my aunts are by the picnic table and clothesline. *They can't still be talking,* I think. *This is a record.* I have never seen them talking this long without eating. Something must really be up.

Mama looks tired. I kneel down on the floor, prop

my chin on the wooden sill, and push the window out slowly until I can hear her voice.

"We've gone around it all night. I think there's still time to send another letter and tell her not to come."

Eva sighs, puts her hands on her hips. "Come on, Maeve. You know her better than any of us. Do you really think that would work? When she wants something, she gets it and no one will stand in her way."

"I can't have her here," Mama says. "What will I tell Georgia?"

Suki speaks up. "Tell Georgia the truth. For God's sake, Maeve, she isn't a baby. She deserves to know."

Eva says something, but I cannot hear. The wind is picking up again. To the west, there are storm clouds. I watch my aunts going back and forth. Suki moves her glasses up and down on the bridge of her nose. She does this whenever she is upset. Then the talking stops and they all look over at the back porch. Grandmother is standing in the doorway. The wind must have awakened her.

"Breakfast?" she asks.

My aunts hurry inside with one last glance at Mama, who remains, battling with the clothespins against the wind, as she takes in laundry. From this height, Mama looks smaller than ever. Her delicate frame makes her appear frail, as if the next strong gust might carry her away.

I decide to stay upstairs. No one will miss me this

morning. They are all too preoccupied. The storm clouds are getting darker. The sky to the north is blue black. Clouds moving fast.

In the distance, I can see a sheet of rain moving toward the house. I open the window wide, pull a chair over, and stand on it. I love to do this. I love to feel the moment the storm hits. I close my eyes and listen. The rain pelts against the barn, the porch roof. The wind whips back my hair. I hold my breath. Cold water hits me hard across the face and I let out a cry.

"Carmen!" I scream it into the wind. I always scream the first word that comes to my mind. Sometimes it's *fear* or *horses* or *silence*. Today I have a feeling of Carmen inside me. A strange, whirling sensation in my stomach I feel whenever Mama and my aunts talk about her. Like being on a ride at the circus that won't stop spinning.

I stand there on the chair until I am thoroughly drenched; then I close the window, peel off all my clothes, and wrap myself in the old crazy quilt on the back of the sofa. Squirt is staring at me. I gather her up in my lap and stroke her black fur. I hear the first echo of Mama's voice calling me down to breakfast as I drift off to sleep.

When I wake, the light is dim. Almost gone. It must be close to five-thirty. The storm has passed for now. I sit up, disturbing Squirt, who stands stunned on her four little paws, considering the situation for a moment before curling up on an old scrap of rug by the hatch. I shuffle to the window, warm in my quilt. Everything outside has been washed clean. I look out to the west and see the lazy motion of a bird. A hawk, I think. Perhaps the same one I have seen circling over the meadow for the past week. A red-tail. It is moving in my direction. As it gets closer, I am not so sure that it is a bird at all. It looks more like one of my aunts, though they wouldn't be out at this time of day. Gradually I can make out long black hair and the thin body of a woman. She is carrying something large in one hand. She circles the upper meadow twice and decends rapidly into the clearing below the pines.

My heart starts racing. There is only one person I know of who would fly in the daylight. I throw off the quilt and open the hatch, climb down, run to my room. I grab a sweatshirt and a pair of jeans, socks from the bedpost. I walk quickly, silently downstairs and into the kitchen.

Mama is standing at the stove, cooking spaghetti. Little red dots cover the front of the apron Grandmother gave her for Christmas last year. CHIEF COOK AND BOTTLE WASHER is printed in black on the front above a picture of a woman elbow deep in suds. Eva says Grandmother gave it to Mama to remind her of her role in the family. As if she could forget. These are the kinds of gifts Grandmother gives, if she gives any at all.

"Georgia, honey. Where have you been hiding all day?" Mama asks, preoccupied with the pot in front of her.

I don't reply. I come up close to her and put my hand on the small of her back. She smells like garlic.

"Mama," I whisper. "She's here."

"Who, Georgia?" she asks cautiously. "Who is here?"

"You know," I say. "Carmen. I saw her land in the clearing."

Mama stares straight ahead at the wall behind the stove.

"Mama?" I am waiting for her to respond. She seems lost for a moment, then snaps to attention.

"Wait for me in the mudroom," she says, untying the apron from around her waist. "I have to think of something to tell your grandmother."

She hurries into the dining room. I go out to the mudroom and slip on the heavy purple-and-blue sweater Suki knitted for Eva a couple of years ago. It has been in the mudroom so long it smells like old geraniums and dampness. Mama joins me. She grabs one of my jackets. All our clothes are interchangeable. Mama takes the Coleman lantern from the hook on the wall and lights it. We slip on our boots and head out.

We climb the small hill that leads to the clearing. The lantern swings before us. I hear Mama breathing, the bark of a dog down in the valley. We are silent. It takes us about twenty minutes to reach the clearing, a circle of flattened grass surrounded by pines.

We hear a woman's voice, humming low and steady. Mama grabs my elbow.

"Georgia, I don't want you to take anything she says seriously. She's like a child. She enjoys playing games. Promise me you won't listen. Promise me, Georgia."

"Sure, Mama," I say. "You know me. I don't listen to anyone."

She smiles. It's dark now so I can't see her, but I can feel her smile. Her grip on my arm loosens. We enter the clearing. There is a dark figure hunched over a small fire. The figure stands up and faces us.

"Ah, the welcoming committee." A laugh. "Maeve, is that you?" The figure walks toward us and Mama holds up the light. "Are you alone, Maeve?"

I step out from behind Mama into the glow of the lantern. Carmen's face comes into the light and I see her for the first time. She could be Mama's twin if Mama had darker skin and had grown to full size. Her hair is long and black and she has no wrinkles around her eyes. The shadow of the lantern plays against her olive complexion, making her beautiful and then hideous. Carmen comes close and places her hand below my chin.

"Beautiful, Maeve, isn't she? Just like we thought."

Mama puts her arm around my waist. I have no

idea what they are talking about, but the hand on my chin makes my skin feel cold.

"Georgia," Carmen says slowly as if she is trying it out for the first time. "Hello, Georgia. I'm your aunt Carmen."

"I know," I say. "I'm the one who saw you land here."

She nods and lets go of my chin, keeping her eyes on my face. Then she turns and moves back to the fire in the clearing.

"I'm going to fly down to the house." Her voice comes out of the darkness. A voice without form speaking to the air. "Will you take my bag?"

Mama doesn't answer.

"My arms are tired. I've been flying since early this morning. There was freezing rain over Toronto. Nasty." She kicks some dirt on the fire, smothering the flames. "Did you tell the old lady I was coming?"

"No," Mama says. "You know how she feels. You'll have to stay in the studio tonight."

"Oh, Maeve. Still trying to hold back the floodwaters. Some things never change."

She starts running without any "Goodbye" or "See you later." She doesn't run far before she is soaring up and over the pines. I walk over to the smoldering fire to pick up the black sack, but Mama calls to me.

"It's late, Georgia. Leave it. She can come back for it herself tomorrow. Bring the lantern, will you?"

Unlike me, Mama dislikes walking home in the

dark. She does not have any native blood running through her tiny veins.

By the time I reach the porch, I can see a light on in the studio on the second floor of the barn. Mama has already gone inside the kitchen. My aunts and Grandmother are seated at the table. I watch them through the glass: Grandmother stiff and serious; Eva waving her arms around her head as she speaks; Suki fingering scales along her napkin; Mama at the stove silently filling her plate with spaghetti.

It is like a play and I am the audience. Not one of them at all. Just someone passing through, walking by their window on a fall evening. Looking in. I feel at moments like this that I don't belong. I've never belonged. Somewhere there must be a missing link that could connect me to them, close the gap between us, if I only knew where to look for it.

I open the back door and walk quietly into the warmth of the kitchen, help myself to a plate of food. I'm starving. I haven't eaten since breakfast.

"Hey, it's about time," says Eva. "We were going to send out a search party if you didn't come soon."

Grandmother casts a disapproving look at Mama. "Really, Maeve. It's bad enough you were out in the evening air with nothing but a thin jacket on, but Georgia has her solo next week. We can't have her getting sick."

Mama looks at me, then at Grandmother. "We needed some mother-daughter time," she says quietly.

Eva and Suki are watching her, but Grandmother has already gone on to the subject of putting hay up for the winter. I think Carmen was wrong when she said things never change. I have the feeling things are already changing.

Chapter 4

It is Monday morning and I'm late. I barely have time to pull on my pants and shirt and grab a piece of toast before Grace honks in the driveway. Grace takes Alice and me to school on her way into town. I swing my backpack into the front seat of Grace's Impala and slam the door after me. You have to slam it hard, because of the rust. I am relieved to be out of the house today. Glad to be going somewhere, even if it's school, instead of waiting around for Grandmother and Carmen to find each other.

Grace and Alice discuss Saturday night's birth, comparing notes about the integrity of the placenta. It is normal Monday-morning conversation. After a while the subject moves to food. Birth or food. Topics with these two are simple and to the point.

First-period English class, Mrs. Browen assigns a 360-page book on the history of the Victorians to be finished in two weeks, and hands back my essay on Emily Brontë. C. Only a C. I'm disappointed. It's not that Mama cares anything about grades. Grandmother either. They care more that I not fly into trees. But I liked this essay. I spent an entire week on it and there is only one comment on the whole thing, in fat red letters. "VAGUE." What's that supposed to mean? Is the whole essay vague or just one part? The facts about Emily Brontë's life *are* rather vague. Besides the fact that she wrote *Wuthering Heights,* there is not much known about her. She spent the last few years of her life in seclusion. I think teachers want history to be more exciting than it really was. They don't want to know that Emily Brontë probably spent her afternoons baking and dusting. They want intrigue, adventure.

In Spanish class we begin with ten minutes of conversation. This morning we are asking each other questions. When it's Carl Snyder's turn he asks, *"¿Se Georgia peina su pelo en las mañanas?"* My face turns red. I want to answer, "Yes, I do comb my hair in the morning. Just not this morning," but I can't put that many Spanish words together all at once.

Carl is small for tenth grade. He has a little bit of facial hair growing on his chin and wears thick reading glasses. He doesn't mean to annoy people, but everything that comes out of his mouth sounds like a whine or a taunt. Usually I just ignore him, smile, and go about my business, but this morning I narrow my eyes and whisper, *"No me molesta ésta mañana, Carlos."* "Don't bother me this morning, Carl."

The morning runs on this way. Five problems wrong on a math test, an incomplete on my watercolor in art class because I left it too close to the heating vents and the edges burned. To top it off, on my way to gym I realize I forgot to put on any underwear. By twelve-thirty I want to go home. I didn't pack a lunch, so Alice gives me half of her smoked Brie and salmon salad and one chocolate éclair.

I sometimes wonder why I even bother coming to school. English is the only class I like, and even there I'm vague. I don't fit here any more than I fit in at home. It's difficult being friends with people you have to lie to. I could tell them some things about myself, but I'd have to make up the rest. I'd have to invent a normal life somehow. Maybe the only place I belong is in the sky or on the back of a horse, where I never have to explain anything.

I arrive home at three o'clock and head directly to my room and comb my hair. It's a warm day for October, so I change out of my turtleneck and slip on a light flannel shirt. I lift the latch on my window. It is one of those big old-fashioned windows with thirty-two panes of glass that opens like a French door. The kind of window I've seen in movies filmed on the Riviera. I was only allowed to move into this room when I turned seven, which Grandmother has declared to be the age of reason. Before this, she said I was too young to have such a big room with a window from which I could fall and break my neck. That never would have happened, though, as I have a great respect for heights and incredible balance. And of course, I can fly.

I hear a voice below me. It's Grandmother yelling up at the roof of the barn. I have seen her do this in the past when pigeons took up residence there. Having pigeons in the barn is one of Grandmother's greatest fears.

"Pigeons in the barn are like bad relatives. They mess up the house, they never leave, and when you go on vacation they invite all of their relations to move in with them."

I don't think she's yelling at pigeons, though, because when Grandmother stops a voice answers back. I lean out the window as far as I can to see what's happening.

On the porch roof that juts out from the studio sits Carmen. Completely naked, sunning herself. Even though it's a warm day for October, I feel cold just looking at her.

"Listen here," Grandmother is saying. "You get yourself off this property or I'll have Sheriff Stone come over here and take you away, clothes or no clothes. Do you hear me?"

"Please," Carmen says. "Could you lower your voice? You are disrupting my meditation." She waves her hand in Grandmother's direction as if she's trying to brush away a fly that has landed on her nose. "Why don't you calm down and I'll set up a time to talk with you later." Carmen lies down on a piece of tie-dyed fabric she must have taken from the wall in the studio and replaces her sunglasses.

I have never heard anyone speak to Grandmother this way. Even the paperboy is afraid of her and calls her "Mrs. Hansen, ma'am." Grandmother's cheeks are turning red. I think she might explode.

"I'm calling the sheriff," She barks up at the roof.

Carmen sits up again, leaving her shades where they are.

"Hey, Vermont is a free state, isn't it? I have the right to sunbathe on my own private property, don't I?"

"That's where you're wrong. This is no private property of yours."

Carmen reaches to her side and pulls over her black bag. She must have retrieved it this morning, or maybe she just put a little spell on it last night and it flew down all on its own. She undoes the drawstring. Her hand disappears inside and emerges with a thick envelope, which she waves in Grandmother's direction.

"I have some business to discuss with you, so why don't you be a nice old gal and meet me at five in the studio?"

Grandmother turns and marches into the house, slamming the screen door behind her. I'm not sure if I should laugh or feel embarrassed for Grandmother. I can't believe Carmen had the power to send her away. Amazing. I am wondering where Suki, Eva, and Mama are when I hear a voice calling up to me. It's Carmen. She has turned in my direction. I have been so absorbed by their argument that I'm leaning far enough out the window to fall on my head, fulfilling Grandmother's prophecy.

I have never seen a woman Carmen's age naked before. I have glimpsed Mama getting out of the shower on occasion, but Carmen looks different. Her breasts are firm and stand straight out from her chest and her stomach is as flat as mine. She's tall and muscular, strong from so many years of flying. I stare.

"Do you always watch the world from up there or do you come down once in a while and check it out for real?"

She pulls a shirt over her head.

"That old lady is a bag of hot air. I don't know how you can stand her. At least you're not afraid of her, though. I can tell. She hasn't taken your power yet, has she? Of course, I've never actually *seen* you fly, but I imagine you can do it, all right. Not like

Maeve. Poor Maeve. I hope you'll take better care of yourself."

I stop staring, feel my face flush. A hot surge of anger rises to my throat. I've had it today. I don't need to listen to this. Who is Carmen, anyway? A stranger. That's all. Just a stranger thinking she knows who I am, who Mama is. I could find a shred of humor in her attitude with Grandmother, but the way she speaks of Mama makes something in my stomach burn.

"Why don't you go back where you came from?" I shout. "Why don't you leave today? No one wants you here." I slam the window, making the glass rattle.

I take the stairs two at a time, jumping over the back stoop and outside, and I run away from the house, down to the ridge. I am so angry I want to punch something, break something. My feet are going on without me. I run faster. I can see the cliff coming up in front of me. I want to stop. I know I should. I try, but my feet won't listen. When I hit the sharp edge of rock, I lie into the air all by myself. I'm not holding on to Eva. I'm not falling into the blackness of night, and I can see everything. Trees and houses and sky. Blue sky. I am flying between sky and earth instead of in a dark, endless void.

I should go back. I should turn around right now and pretend it never happened, but I can't think clearly. I am so full of anger. "Damn you, Carmen," I yell. "Damn you for making me do this." But Carmen isn't around to hear me. I can't hear myself as the air rushes past my ears, and my eyes are stunned by the beauty of the sky. I fly on.

I try to keep my focus, concentrate on my breathing like Eva taught me, put the image of Carmen inside a small box at the back of my brain, but my anger keeps bubbling up, so I let it. Let it propel me forward.

I head down the valley to the little red farmhouse I have seen so many times from the ridge. I watch the afternoon sun reflect off the silver silo, turning it into a gleaming tower. I want to get closer but I don't dare. It is bad enough that I am breaking the rules and will probably never be allowed to solo; I don't want to be seen on top of that. Maybe I should keep going and never come back. What's there to come home to, anyway? Grandmother's anger? School? Carmen? My own banishment?

I take a deep breath, increase my altitude, and fly as far away from the house as possible.

I fly south over the Hopkins cornfield, over the crisp stalks and the Hopkinses' horse, Brandy, who has jumped the fence again and is eating a patch of grass that is still long and green. Brandy is an old mare but she can jump any fence if there is something on the other side she wants badly enough. Brandy was the first horse I ever rode. Bud Hopkins used to let me ride her around his barn whenever

Mama and I went over to buy eggs. I have never seen Brandy from this perspective before. She looks small. I yell down, "Hey, Brandy," but she can't hear me. She's not used to looking up. Most animals—and people—are not.

I decide to keep to the more rural areas. I could cause quite a commotion if I flew over the village of Hawthorne at this hour of the afternoon and someone *did* look up. I fly south toward the islands, where Eva never lets me go. There is a hydroelectric plant on the mainland near St. Simon. Eva's afraid I'll get too close out of curiosity and get caught in the power lines, but I have no desire to go there. I only want to see the water. I'll stay on this side of St. Simon. There is a good strong wind, blowing me in that direction. Out over the waters of Lake Champlain.

More than ten thousand years ago, Lake Champlain was an inland sea connected to the Atlantic Ocean by the St. Lawrence Seaway. Divers have found the skeleton of a whale in the lake, and there are rumors that a sea monster still lives in the depths. It does look deep and mysterious from up here when the shadows of the clouds pass across it. It's bordered by the cold, gray Adirondack mountains rising to the west. There is a bit of snow on a few of the higher peaks, like little white hats.

From the air, St. Simon looks smaller than it seemed last summer when I picked blueberries there with Mama. It is a fifteen-minute ferry ride from the mainland, in summer. No ferries go to St. Simon in the fall, so there is no chance of anyone seeing me here. Even if they did, they would only mistake me for a gull.

It is not a bad day for flying, but over water, the air currents are more fierce and less predictable. I attempt to head north, but the wind picks up and I'm blown farther south. I make an adjustment. This is what Eva calls it when the weather forces you to change plans. "You have to always be willing to change your mind, Georgia. Don't get rigid in your thinking about how it should be up there. There is nothing in the sky that can't change in an instant." I pull my arms down to my sides in an effort to descend, but within a minute I'm blown in the direction of the mainland. There is nothing I can do. I can't fight the wind, so I have to wait for it to change.

Below me, the hydroelectric plant comes into view, but I'm too afraid to look down. I have to move away as quickly as possible and stay above the power lines. Getting anywhere near them could be deadly. I feel a slight buzz inside my mouth. My metal fillings are picking up current. Suki has told me if I ever feel that sensation, I am too close to a source of electricity and I should increase my altitude and fly straight home.

I can see the dam directly ahead. Fear grabs hold of me as the image of Charlotte's gravestone comes to my mind. Cold slate like the color of the dam.

Charlotte flew alone before initiation, and look what happened to her. "For the one who flew too high. Dear Lord Have Mercy."

"Please," I pray. "Please. Not like Charlotte."

If someone had told me I'd be flying alone over Lake Champlain in the daylight, I never would have believed them. There was no way this morning I could have known where the afternoon would bring me.

Like Charlotte. She woke up that morning with only one thought in her mind. Skating. Skating with her father. She dressed, brushed her teeth, and kissed Isadora goodbye without much thought. Without any knowledge that it would be the last time. It makes me shiver when I think how unpredictable life is. How just when you think you have everything in order, you break your arm or fall off a mountain or get sucked into some power lines.

Up here those thoughts only fill me with fear, and in the sky fear is your worst enemy. I breathe in deeply and try to recall Eva's words instead. We were flying in a hailstorm last spring and Eva told me, "You may not know what's ahead of you, Georgia. The weather could be better. It could be worse. But you can't get stuck in the place of fear. You have to feel the fear, let it pass through you, and keep going. You have to be brave."

I breathe deeply and feel the fear tingling down my arms. I climb higher, and within a minute the wind changes in my favor, blows me east back over the lake. I fly home. It takes me about ten minutes to reach the ridge. I approach from the north, where there is less chance of someone seeing me. I expect the whole family to be standing out there waiting, but there isn't anyone in sight and at this point I no longer care because all I can think of is that I'm alive and I've been given a second chance.

Chapter 5

This time of year the barn smells sweet from the hay Mr. Gowen brings in for the winter. We don't need the hay. We have no animals to feed. But Grandmother likes the hay put up just in case. In case of what, I do not know.

The one thing Grandmother did not take into consideration with her "no men" rule was how to move tractors and hay the fields and repair the plumbing with a house full of artistic women. Perhaps she hoped one of us would show more of an interest in things mechanical. In any event, she has to hire people to take care of practical matters. She spends a great deal of her time supervising and scheduling the hired help. She refers to them as "the people." She'll say, "I have good people who work for me," or "It's hard to find people to come out here."

"Where are my people today?" she'll ask frantically when Mr. Gowen, the handy man, or T. C. Pelman, the plumber, is late for mowing or haying or any of the hundred odd jobs Grandmother has lined up for one of her "people" to do.

I've known Mr. Gowen for as long as I can remember. In fact, Mr. Gowen and T. C. Pelman are the only men in my life except for my science teacher, Mr. Howard. Mr. Howard is old enough to be my father, but not as accessible as Mr. Gowen. Mr. Howard is married and has four children and lives in a big house over in Garrison. I think he already has too many commitments, too many women who expect to be special to him as it is. He doesn't need another. Mr. Gowen is different. When I'm with him, I can just be myself, and no matter what I do or say it seems to please him.

I hear Beulah coming down the driveway. Grandmother spends every Monday afternoon sorting books for the Hawthorne Historical Society. She always arrives home irritable, complaining of a stiff neck from looking down for so many hours in the society's damp basement.

It is ten minutes to five. I need to take my place if I want to hear anything of Carmen and Grandmother's conversation. I haven't seen Carmen since I came back. I went directly to my room and fell asleep for half an hour, took a shower, and stroked Squirt's fur until she'd had enough of it and hid under my bed.

Whenever I'm worried, I pet Squirt long and hard. Right now I'm worried about Carmen. I'm worried she saw me take off and is going to tell Grandmother.

There is a loose floorboard in the studio on the second floor of the barn that opens a long crack in the ceiling below. I climb up on the hay bales, feel around with my hands until I find it. I give it a shove, and dust and hayseed fall into my hair and eyes. If Grandmother knew about this board being loose, Mr. Gowen would be called in to fix it, which is why I've never told her. I keep it jammed up tight whenever I'm not using it as my spy hole. I found it one day when I was helping Mr. Gowen stack hay. I stood up and hit my head so hard on it the board gave way. It's been giving way ever since. The floorboards are getting old.

Great-grandfather built the studio at the turn of the century as his invention room. The Cooney Clasp was made there. It is the only invention he made any money on, though I don't think he did it for money. Making things was just something he had to do. He invented hundreds of impractical gadgets, some finished, others lying in boxes on the first floor of the barn. My favorite is the egg cracker: an eggcup with a tiny hammer attached to the side by a spring. When you draw back the hammer with your fingers and let go, it cracks the egg into the cup. I've used it a couple of times. It needs some adjustment, as the egg usually misses the cup and oozes down the side.

Grandmother never mentions any of Great-grandfather's other creative attempts. She never mentions anything about her father, other than his success, which seems a little narrow-minded to me.

I prop my back up against a hay bale and pull a package of malt balls from my pocket. It's too dark to make out the ingredients on the back label, but I believe they have absolutely no nutritional value, which makes me very happy.

I see Carmen's bare feet walk across the studio floor to the sink. She turns on a light and sits down at the table. I have an excellent view from here. I can see everything but Carmen's left arm, which disappears into the shadows. I stare up at her face. It is a long, thin face with an elegant nose. She's very attractive, sensual in a way, comfortable inside her own skin. I wonder if there is a look to a person who breaks the rules, a strength in the jaw, a knowing in the eyes like Carmen has. I wonder if I look different now. If I look more like her. If I *am* more like her. She seems softer tonight, less fierce, but still unpredictable. Someone I don't trust.

I wish I were still angry with Carmen. It would make things easier. I'm not sure what I feel toward her. All I know is I'm glad to be alive and that seems to overshadow everything else at this moment—except my worry over her telling. As much as I would like to be free of Grandmother's rules, I don't want to be sent away like Carmen. I don't want to leave before I'm ready. I get an empty feeling in my belly whenever I think about never seeing this place or Mama or Suki or Eva again. There's so much to lose.

When I was little and Mama told me the story of Carmen's banishment, I always wondered what I would do, where I would go, if I made some irreparable mistake. Even then, it seemed unfair to me that Grandmother had that much control over our lives. Now here I am at that place. My future is in the hands of a woman I hardly know. I think Carmen might be trying to help me in her own strange way, but I also think she could be out to destroy me. With her knowledge of my forbidden solo, she could do either.

Carmen empties a leather pouch onto the table and a handful of small stones fall out. She turns them over and closes her eyes. Then carefully she picks one, flips it, and holds it in her hand.

"Patience," she says, and sighs. Runes, I think that's what they're called. Grace has a set she keeps in an old cookie tin on her nightstand. Once in a while she takes the runes out and washes them in a pot in the kitchen sink until they are smooth and dark. Sometimes she asks Alice and me to think of a question and pick a stone out of the water. I almost always choose the one with the arrow. Courage.

At a little past five Grandmother's footsteps ascend the stairs to the studio and Carmen collects the stones and drops them back into the pouch. I practice controlling my breath. *Breathe, breathe, hold.* Thank goodness I'm not allergic to hay.

There is no exchange of greetings when Grandmother enters the studio. She is very good at the silent treatment. I can see her face, like a stone. Her body rigid, wearing a gray apron and practical shoes. Carmen dressed in black silks and gold jewelry. I can hear the dozen bracelets on her arms jangling. Chairs scrape the floor.

"I want you to look at these." It's Carmen's voice.

The sound of paper being placed on the table. Silence. Paper moving. I crane my neck so my ear is as close to the opening in the board as it can be.

"I don't see how this has anything to do with me." Grandmother's voice is sharp.

"It is a copy of the will," Carmen explains slowly. "I recently searched through some old records and discovered that when Isadora died she divided the property evenly among us. She left me the barn, the studio, and twelve acres on the east hill. I know you have never told the others."

Grandmother pushes her chair out and stands up. "Is this why you've come back? To disrupt our lives? Didn't you do enough damage the last time?"

I see Carmen's back lean deeper into the chair. "It all depends on what you call damage. It looks like you made a fine recovery. You did get Georgia out of the deal, after all."

When she says my name, I shiver.

"Georgia is none of your business. You agreed to that when you left."

"Don't worry. I'm not here for Georgia. I came only for the initiation, as we agreed sixteen years ago. I know you hoped I would forget." She hands something to Grandmother. "This is my birthday gift to Georgia. I'm giving her the land deeded to me on the east hill. I've already had it taken care of by my lawyer in San Francisco." There is a pause.

"It is very generous of you to give away something that isn't yours," says Grandmother.

"It *is* mine," says Carmen. There is anger in her voice. "No matter what little tricks you've played, Mother, I know the truth. I have the papers. I'm giving Georgia her freedom."

Grandmother turns and walks out of the studio. I can hear her firm steps down the stairs and the snap of the back door. Carmen sighs. I am confused. Why would Grandmother withhold land from us, and why would Carmen give anything to me? What is this agreement they are talking about?

Carmen takes a box of matches from the shelf above the stove, lights a stick of incense, and circles her head with it twice. She walks over to the door and blows smoke all around the edges of the frame as if to seal off cracks where air could seep in. As if to keep out any unwanted spirits from coming in the night.

Chapter 6

I spend Tuesday after school with Suki. Along with her many other talents, Suki is a seamstress. She has delicate fingers like Mama's and great patience. Suki is helping me with my initiation dress. All the Hansen women keep their dresses, packed safely away in boxes. They are cared for like wedding gowns. I have seen Eva's and Suki's. They are exotic. Black fabric decorated with fine glass beads and fringe hanging at the sleeves or hem, but they are not old-fashioned. *Otherworldly* is a better description. Suki's dress is tiered. Four layers of black silky tassels cover the front, and it falls just above the ankle. Eva's is simpler, more elegant. They are meant to be beautiful and also practical for flying. Both dresses have long slits that reach to the thigh for easy maneuvering.

The initiate makes her own dress with the help of her aunt or her mother. It can take a year to complete, but it must be done before the initiate's sixteenth birthday. I am almost done with mine.

My initiation ceremony will begin with a bonfire and a blessing in the clearing at dusk on Thursday. I will fly with a partner to the ridge and then alone to the Missisquoi Wildlife Reserve five miles to the north, and back. I will be sleeping in the reserve for a few hours to prove I can survive in the woods and also to rest for the flight home. Eva says it's important to know you can survive if you're ever grounded by bad weather, and flying alone takes double the energy when you're first starting because you're doing all the navigation as well. It's important to rest and clear your head when you can. I am allowed to bring a sleeping bundle, matches for a fire, and a candle. Nothing else. When I return, just before dawn, there will be a celebration with food and music. Following the solo, I will be able to fly alone at night with only minimum supervision for six months. After that I will be free to go as far and as high as I wish.

Only one thing stands in my way, and that is Grandmother finding out about my flight yesterday afternoon. If Grandmother knew I flew alone before initiation, all my privileges would be taken away. There would be no celebration and I would be asked to leave the family. Even if Carmen doesn't tell Grandmother, I still have to make it through the ceremony and answer the question "Have you waited until your sixteenth birthday to fly unattended in the sky?" How will I answer this? Will I lie to stay on Grandmother's good side? To be fed and clothed and housed? Or will I tell the truth?

Today Suki is finishing the hem on my dress and I am embroidering a tiny horse onto the front of the sash. Suki gave me gold, brown, and rust-colored thread to stand out against the black material. I've already stitched the body and legs. Now I'm working on the head. Suki says it's good luck to stitch a dream or wish into your initiation dress.

"You know, Georgia, this will be the most important day of your life, the first time you fly alone." I look down at the sash in my lap. My face feels hot. I hope she can't read my mind.

"I remember my initiation clearly. My birthday is in June, as of course you know. The weather was beautiful. Your mama helped me with my dress and swept my hair up in a twist. I wore Great-grandmother's long silver-and-onyx earrings. I even had black gloves." She laughs. "I felt like the most beautiful woman in the world."

"Tell me about the owl," I say. I want Suki to keep talking. I want to hear her calm voice telling me stories so I won't have to think about myself for a while. The owl story is my favorite.

"Georgia, you've heard this so many times."

"No, come on, please," I beg.

"Okay." She clears her throat. "The owl." She takes a minute to remember.

"Well, we were all up in the clearing for the ceremony. Mother, Eva, Maeve, and you, Georgia, standing around the bonfire singing. Do you remember it?" I nod. I was eight at the time and Suki's ceremony was magic in my memory.

"Mother gave the blessing and I started to leave. That year it was decided that I wouldn't fly with anyone, I would walk down to the cliff alone. Maeve hadn't flown since you were born, Eva had a bad cold that filled her ears with fluid and set her off balance, and Mother had to stay and finish the ritual. I understand now why it's important to have someone walk or fly with you to the ridge, so you can talk instead of being alone with your fear.

"I was nervous as I walked away by myself. Afraid of the dark all of a sudden. I thought, *What if I can't do it?* Just for a second. But still, it shook me. There I was walking off to the cliff filled with doubt.

"I turned around to go back to the fire and tell Mother I wasn't ready yet. I walked about five feet when a rush of feathers came down from above. A great horned owl swooped from one of the pines and landed at my feet. He was huge. His head turned back and forth and his eyes glowed. He just sat there. I waved my hands at him, but he wouldn't fly away. I tried to walk around him, but he moved to block me. He didn't want me to go back. He didn't want me to follow my fear. For a second, I had this image in my mind of Isadora making the wooden owl that sits on the barn roof to scare away the pigeons. She worked on it every day for a whole month. I could see her face and hands as she carved the wings. I could smell her and hear the little carving knife chipping away at the block of wood. She was a determined woman. When she had carved enough, she took one of the big ladders from the barn, climbed up to the roof, and nailed that owl down to the old weathervane stand. She stood on the ladder next to her owl and smiled, and in my memory it seemed like she was smiling at me. A feeling of complete calm came over me then and I knew I would be fine. I turned around and walked toward the ridge and the owl flew back up into the trees. I ran right off the cliff that night like I'd always done, practicing with Mother. And I've been doing it ever since."

We both sit in the quiet for a minute. The image of Suki running off the cliff plays again in my mind. I feel suddenly guilty. Let down. Maybe it won't be the same for me now that I've already done it. Maybe I'll be disappointed with the dark now that I've flown in the light.

"I love that story," I say. "It sounds like a dream."

"It was like a dream," says Suki.

I look down at the horse head I've been sewing. My hand is beginning to cramp up from holding the tiny needle so tightly. Suki reaches over and places her hand on my knee.

"You'll be fine, Georgia. Don't worry. It'll be the best day of your life. You'll have your own stories to tell soon."

I nod. "I know." I give her a weak smile. "It's time for me to fly now."

Suki tells me the dress needs a few more hours of work. We agree to meet tomorrow to finish up. She hangs the dress on a silk hanger on the back of her closet door.

The days are so short now. I can feel winter. It is a clear night, though cold, and I promised to meet Eva in her room before we go flying. We only have two more nights to practice before my birthday. Tonight Eva is taking me to the river, to the spot I'll be flying to on Thursday.

I stop in my room and pull on a black turtleneck, exchange my jeans for long underwear and black corduroys, pull a black knit hat over my ears.

Eva's room is tucked away in the farthest corner of the second floor. I don't come down here very often because this is where Eva paints and she doesn't like to be disturbed. She used to paint in the studio, but she says the light in her room is better and she has a clear view of the valley. I knock lightly on her door. The smells of perfume and oil paint drift out from the crack at the bottom and up into my nostrils.

"Come in, Georgia," Eva calls.

I open the door. The dark hallway is illuminated.

I love Eva's room. It's the most beautiful room in the house. Not only because it's spacious and filled with light but because it has the cupola. One wall filled with windows that bows out into the branches of a giant maple tree. When I was little and Mama read me the story of Rapunzel, I always imagined Rapunzel's tower looking exactly like Eva's room and Grandmother looking exactly like the witch who kept her there.

Eva's room is full of color. This month the walls are painted tangerine with avocado trim. There are so many coats of paint on her walls that the room appears to be getting smaller with each new inspiration of color. Eva says she's leaving the tangerine for a while. It's the best shade she's had so far. There are canvases in various stages of completion lined up along one wall. Eva has covered her current canvas with a white sheet. She doesn't like anyone to watch her paint. She thinks it's bad luck.

"Let me put these things away, honey, and I'll be right with you."

While Eva puts her brushes to soak in an old tin can, I look at her paintings. She paints landscapes. Fields, barns, sky. The way the magenta, gold, and indigo are swirled together, everything appears to be moving. Her landscapes look like they are on fire. Like the green fields and mountains of Vermont have been caught up in a blaze of motion and color.

"Okay, Georgia. I'm ready." Eva sighs. She loves flying in the spring and summer, but when the weather turns cold, she would rather stay in and paint. I know she's coming just for me. She promised, and Eva always keeps her promises.

Halfway downstairs, Eva says she forgot to screw the caps back on her tubes of oil paint and I tell her I'll meet her at the cliff.

On my way, I meet Carmen. She is walking over to the house, lost in thought. Having just eavesdropped on her private conversation makes me feel awkward. I wonder what business she has at the house or even if she is allowed inside, but since Carmen follows no rules except her own, how could she possibly break any?

"Nice flying," she says. "Yesterday afternoon. Extremely graceful."

I stare at her, shocked that she would be so bold. *Why hasn't she told Grandmother yet?* I wonder. She's playing with me. That's what she's doing. She wants to get a rise out of me again. Make me do something even more reckless this time. My anger returns, climbs like hot little fingers over each of my ribs, moving up to my throat, but I stop it before I blurt out words I don't want to give her. Words I'd have to pay for later. I pretend I don't know what she's talking about. I give her a blank look. There is a chance that even if she did tell, no one would believe her.

Carmen glances over my shoulder. Eva is coming.

I can hear her ankle bracelets jangling and smell her perfume. She orders it special from a catalog in Minnesota. I will forever associate flying with the smell of Eva's Paris Passion.

"Carmen," Eva says flatly.

"Eva," Carmen replies.

I have always assumed Eva and Suki had little interest in Carmen, but I can tell there is some tension between them.

"I was just saying what a graceful flier Georgia must be," Carmen says. "A natural."

"Yes," says Eva, smiling at me. "She is a good student."

"And beautiful, too," Carmen adds. I narrow my eyes at her.

Eva elbows me. "Say thank you, Georgia," she encourages.

"Thank you, Georgia," I say. Carmen laughs.

"I'd like to fly with you one day," Carmen says. She emphasizes the word *day*. I look over at Eva, but there is no sign she suspects anything.

"Suit yourself," I reply.

"Maybe I will," says Carmen. "But not tonight. I'm busy tonight."

"Fine," I say. "Let's go, Eva." I grab Eva's hand. I want to get away from Carmen before she says anything more. I do not trust her. Just because she didn't tell Grandmother doesn't mean she wouldn't tell Eva. I see now what Mama means about Carmen playing games. We are like little chess pieces to her. Rooks and bishops she can move around and knock over as the mood strikes her.

Maybe Carmen is going to the house to find Mama and tell her how I broke the rules. She wants me to join her. That's it. She's tired of being the only outcast in the family and wants company. Maybe she planned this before she came. She probably has a little room all ready for me in her cottage by the sea. Well, I won't go with her. I'll go live with Grace and Alice instead.

Carmen is staring at me. "Wandering off in thought?" she asks.

I close my lips tight.

"Good night, Carmen," says Eva.

"Good night, sister," says Carmen.

* * *

Tonight Eva wants me to take off without holding her hand. A couple of nights ago, I would have been afraid to do this, but after yesterday, I have more confidence. I nod.

"Do you feel ready, honey?"

"I'll have to do it on Thursday night. I could use the practice."

"Good girl!" Eva smiles. "Now, remember. Don't think with your head. Take off from your belly." She pats her own. "I'll be right next to you. Let's go."

We both start running. Side by side. When we hit

the edge I lie into the air fine, just like I did yesterday. I hear Eva give a little cry of excitement and it startles me. For the past few flying sessions, we've been silent. Eva wants me to get used to flying alone. I'm not allowed to ask questions unless it's an emergency. I'm supposed to figure things out on my own. I can tell Eva is pleased with my confidence tonight. She stays a little behind me, watching. When we reach the pines, she veers to the right, in the direction of the river. I follow.

The air is cold, rushing past my cheeks. We circle twice, and on the second pass Eva points to a small lake beneath us. This is where I'll be going on Thursday. We won't land there tonight. There have to be some surprises when I'm on my own, some test of my skill, and Eva knows landings are my weak point, the only time I start thinking with my head.

I reach out and hold Eva's hand, give it a squeeze so she knows I understand where to land. I'm excited about flying alone, but I'll miss flying with Eva. There is a closeness I feel to her when we're in the air that I don't when we're home. Up in the sky things are a little less certain. We rely on one another and it draws us closer. I can't fly with Mama, of course, but I can still fly with Eva and Suki whenever I want to. I guess I could even fly with Grandmother, though that's not something that crosses my mind very often. Grandmother only flies on rare occasions, to keep herself in practice. She'll take off in the middle of the night and come home long before dawn. Always alone.

I've only seen her in the air once. I was about nine years old. I woke up during a storm and she was circling the house. The wind was blowing the sleeves of her black shirt straight out behind her, making her look like some kind of prehistoric bird. I was afraid she was going to crash through my window, pick me up with her talons, and fly away with me, but she just landed awkwardly on top of the picnic table, brushed off her skirt, and walked inside.

Eva rolls over once and I copy her move. That's her sign to head home. I can tell by the way she turns her face away from the wind that she wants to get back to her painting.

Chapter 7

Overnight the temperature has dropped, and a heavy frost covers the garden. It amazes me that the Swiss chard and kale are standing tall and green and the pumpkins bright orange under a coat of white, while all the other vegetables are rotting and brown at their feet.

I woke up this morning with the most delicious feeling of freedom. No school. Today or tomorrow. I am allowed to stay home to finish my dress, help with final preparations for my initiation, and relax, although Grandmother is not big on the relaxation part of this equation. Before leaving for Burlington to visit her lawyer early this morning, she wrote down a long list of things for me to do, which she posted on the refrigerator. The first chore is TAKE OUT COMPOST. I take out the compost every morning, so it's not necessary to put it on any list, but Grandmother does not like to leave anything to chance.

The compost bin is next to the pumpkin patch. My leather shoes are quickly covered with flakes of white. It's time for snow, but this year I'm not ready. I do not want to solo in a blizzard. Flying through a snowstorm is much more frightening than driving through one. It can be deadly if you don't know where you are. There is no moon to guide you. You can fly too low. You can get close to a silo or a stand of pines, to electrical wires.

The sound of a truck coming down the driveway shakes me from my thoughts. It is rare where we live to have visitors. The only people who come on any regular basis are the workmen Grandmother hires. From the sound of the engine, I'd say it is Mr. Gowen. His truck makes a little *putt-putt* like the engine of a Volkswagen bug.

The noise of the engine grows louder and Mr. Gowen's red truck appears from behind the giant willow tree at the bend in the road. He brought his dog, Duke, today. Duke is a big old hound dog. Standing in the bed of the truck trying to keep his balance, Duke is wearing a bright fluorescent orange vest. It is tied around him with baling twine. It's hunting season and no dog is safe, not even here. Grandmother posted our land ten years ago, and Mr. Gowen replaces the signs with a new warning each year. NO HUNTING OR TRAPPING ON THESE PREMISES. It doesn't seem to make much of a difference, though. There were generations of families hunting on this land long before a Hansen ever bought it.

Beginning in October, hunters walk the border of the meadow. They park their pickups at the end of the road. Grandmother tries to stop them every year, sending poor Mr. Gowen out to talk to them. I bet he just tells them to keep a safe distance from the house or to come back on Saturday when the old lady isn't home.

I'm glad I'll have soloed before rifle season starts. There is no danger in the air at night, but I'll be sleeping in the reserve and there is a chance of duck hunters just before dawn. Since I eat ham sandwiches, I guess I shouldn't judge hunters, but it always makes me shiver, the thought of shooting any winged creature out of the sky.

I place the compost bucket on the porch and wave to Mr. Gowen.

"Sweet Georgia Brown!" he yells out the window, extending his long, lanky arm. He parks the truck and cuts the engine. Duke stands in back, his mournful face staring at me.

"Come over here and let me look at you, girl." I walk over. "Turn around. Ooh, what a sight. Makes me want to cry to see such beauty before these tired old eyes."

Mr. Gowen's eyes are large and sparkling and not

at all tired. I laugh and give him a soft punch on the sleeve of his flannel shirt.

"Frost is on the pumpkins, Georgia Brown."

"I know, Mr. Gowen," I say, frowning.

"What's the matter, honey? You don't like the snow? Not becoming a flatlander, are you? Gonna fly to Flor-i-da first sign of a flake? Go live with the old folks?"

"Maybe," I say. "Maybe I'll fly south with the geese one year and I won't ever come back to Nowhere, Vermont."

"You know, I don't think you're so sweet after all. I'm gonna start calling you Sour Georgia Brown."

"That's okay by me," I say.

He shakes his head and picks at his bottom teeth with a toothpick. "Old lady around?" he asks, lowering his voice. He gets out of the truck, walks to the back, and lets Duke out.

"No," I say. "She had to go down to Burlington on some business."

"Good. Good. 'Cause I got some news for you."

"Really, what?" I ask.

"I hear Emmett Fogg's got a gelding he don't want."

"How come he doesn't want it? What's wrong with it?" I ask.

"Hold on to your pants, girl. Don't go finding fault where there ain't none. Nothing wrong with it. A beauty. I seen it. Emmett's stable is booked. No room. Maybe he'll let you take him for the winter. You got space in the barn. Lord knows you got plenty of first-cut hay. Fogg won't let you take him unless he knows you can care for him right."

"Can I see him?" I ask.

Mr. Gowen looks around, whispers. "What about school? What's the old lady gonna say?"

"I don't have to go to school today and Grandmother won't say anything. She's not here. I just want to look, Mr. Gowen. Please, will you take me?"

"I'll take you, honey," he laughs. "After I fix the gate."

I bring in the compost bucket, put it by the sink, and run upstairs. My room is a mess. I dig out a pair of riding jeans and boots from the bottom of my closet, extra socks, a plaid shirt. I return to the kitchen, grab a basket of carrot muffins from the counter, and head out to the truck.

I wait for Mr. Gowen to finish. I know he didn't come all the way out here just to fix the gate. He usually waits until Grandmother has accumulated half a dozen odd jobs, then puts them together and makes one trip. He came to tell me about the horse. Ever since I was a little girl, Mr. Gowen has been coming out here, taking me for rides to see horses and feeding me chocolates. I have attended every horse show in the Mad River Valley, thanks to Mr. Gowen, who drives me all the way down there so I can smell that smell. Horses and new hay. The smell of wildness and freedom.

"That was quick," I say as Mr. Gowen eases himself into the seat next to me. He is a tall, wiry man with a slightly crooked spine, so his right leg is shorter than his left. He has a thick wave of salt-and-pepper hair that sweeps across the top of his head, long black sideburns, and gentle blue eyes.

"I'm leaving Duke here until we get back. That nose of his will only get him into trouble around the stables." He reaches over and picks up a muffin. "Ah, some squirrel food." Mr. Gowen thinks we eat like rodents, picking at our seeds and nuts. He takes a bite of the muffin and starts the truck.

"That grandmother of yours has me out here for the smallest of jobs. Things you could do, or one of your pretty aunts."

I notice he doesn't suggest Mama. It is well known that Mama is not in a position to be fixing things or lifting heavy objects. She is allowed to cook, but even then I have to help her take down the heavy cast-iron skillets from their hooks above the woodstove.

"You know what the trouble is? There ain't no men around here. Never have been. I don't understand why Myra"—he clears his throat—"why the old lady doesn't have any on board."

I shrug my shoulders. "Who knows? No men. No horses." I turn my head and watch the fields pass by outside the truck window. Brown and dry. Waiting to be covered in their winter blanket. "Has she always been like that, Mr. Gowen?"

"Afraid so, honey. At least as long as I've known her. She's a little on the tight side. I always thought it had to do with your great-grandmother. She was a hard woman, single-minded. Ran this place like an army barracks. I guess the old feller was too busy to do anything besides make those crazy inventions of his, so the work fell to her and then in the end he got all the recognition." He stops then like he's said too much. "Ain't none of my business no more, honey." He finishes his muffin, wipes his mouth on his sleeve. "So what do you think you'll do with this gelding, if you get him? Where you gonna keep him? In your room? Up in the widow's peak?" He chuckles.

"The widow's walk," I correct him. "I have some ideas," I say.

Mr. Gowen hums a little. He puts the truck into fourth gear and it gives a little jerk. "Yep. What you ladies need out here is a permanent man."

* * *

Emmett Fogg's place is outside the village of Garrison. One hundred acres of rolling hills, pasture, a farmhouse, and stables enough for a dozen horses. I drove by once when Eva and I came out here to press cider with my kindergarten class, up the street at Ralph Reimann's. Ralph was the richest kid in my school. The Reimanns invited the whole class to try out their new cider press on the back lawn that day. They live in a beautiful brick farmhouse with a porch wrapping around most of it, little stone pathways that lead to gardens in the woods. Gardens with springs and statues of the Buddha or marble gargoyles staring down into their own reflections beside small fountains.

Ralph's parents are artists. His mother travels to New York every other week to check on her paintings in galleries. She is a tall, thin, glamorous woman with blunt-cut hair that frames her face. She is not beautiful in the way I am used to a woman being beautiful. She is angular and severe in her loose-fitting silk pants and blousy shirts. She stands out in the corner market down the road with her bright red lipstick, smelling of oil paint and expensive cologne.

Ralph's father, on the other hand, is a shy, awkward man, balding and stocky. He could be an ordinary Vermonter with his worn shirts and work boots, until he opens his mouth. He has a thick German accent and a slight lisp. He sculpts statuary, angels, lions, goddesses.

I always thought Ralph was lucky. He had both his parents and they were always doing things together. I never saw Ralph without one of them when he was little. He never seemed lonely. Never. I told Eva this once and she said, "You can never tell, Georgia, if someone is lonely or not. Just because Ralph has a family that's still together doesn't mean he never gets lonely. Maybe he would rather change places with you."

"I doubt it," I told Eva.

Maybe it was the way Mrs. Reimann always scooped Ralph up in her arms like he was the most delicious thing she'd ever seen or the fact that Mr. Reimann held his wife's hand in public, but they all seemed to fit together nicely.

It was a freezing October day, the day Eva and I went to the Reimanns'. Eva wore a silk dress with leather flats, which got all wet from the dew on the grass. She was miserable. I could tell by the way she held her lips together too tightly. Her hair started to kink in the rain, and Eva hates her hair to get kinky. She will do almost anything to prevent it, including wearing rags soaked in olive oil on her head all night long. There wasn't much she could do about it that day, though.

I thought Eva had dressed up just to accompany me on my first field trip. Now I know it was because she wanted Mrs. Reimann's opinion of her paintings. She figured she had one chance to meet her, so she piled eight canvases in the back of Beulah. They never got around to talking about art, though, because Ralph's index finger got caught in the barrel of the cider press and he had to be whisked away to the medical center in Burlington, leaving us all standing around with Mrs. Johnson, our kindergarten teacher, who spent an hour explaining to us how dangerous cider presses can be.

I cannot see the Reimanns' place from the road. Like most of the houses in this part of Garrison, it's hidden in the trees at the end of a long driveway.

Mr. Gowen has turned on WWRK, the country station. Tammy Wynette is belting out a song.

"How can you stand that kind of music, Mr. Gowen?" I ask him.

"I love it, honey. Why, country music is the only music where you can lose your lover, your dog, your house, and your car all in the course of one song. Makes my life not seem so hard. Course you don't know about that yet. You're too young to have it hard."

I roll my eyes. "That's what you think," I say.

Mr. Gowen smiles. He smiles a lot. He seems completely unaware that he is missing three teeth in the front of his mouth. He just keeps opening it wide. One of his most endearing qualities.

We pull into the long driveway of the Fogg Stables and park in the wide horseshoe-shaped parking lot.

"Well, Sour Georgia, let's see what we can see."

Emmett Fogg is standing at the entrance of the stables. He seems surprised to see us, like he was expecting someone else. His arms are folded across his broad chest. He is tall and forbidding, dark. He nods as we approach. "Gowen," he says.

Mr. Gowen looks at the ground, suddenly shy. "This is the girl," he mumbles.

I look at him, horrified. "This is the girl?" It sounds like he wants Mr. Fogg to check my flanks and consider me for a place in one of his stalls. *This is how you introduce me to a man who owns a horse I desperately want?* I think. I step forward and extend my hand. "I'm Georgia Hansen."

Emmett Fogg does not take it. He looks over my head and turns to the stables. "The horse is in here," he says over his shoulder as he walks away. "You can go in yourself, have a look. I have to make a call. He's the fourth stall on the right."

"Friendly sort, isn't he?" Mr. Gowen whispers. I give him a look. I haven't forgiven him yet for his poor introduction.

We enter the stable. It's beautiful, with a large tack room. I glance inside at the saddles and harnesses neatly hung on the walls while Mr. Gowen finds the stall.

"Over here, Georgia Brown."

The name RUSTY is printed in large block letters on an index card, held by a thumbtack. I see that all the other horses have brass nameplates adorning the front of their stalls. It is clear that Rusty was never intended for a long stay at the Fogg Stables. He puts his head over the door of the stall. A large, gentle, elegant head. I can tell at first glance that he is definitely not a Rusty, a name given by someone who did not know this horse. He is more of a rich nut color. Like one of those old photographs tinged in brown. Sepia. I look over at Mr. Gowen.

"What did I tell you? Isn't he a beauty?" He pulls a carrot out of his pocket. He knew I'd jump at a chance for a horse like this. So sure of it he filled his pockets with carrots.

Emmett Fogg comes inside. He is carrying a cellular phone. He stands behind me.

"You think you can handle him? Gowen informs me you can ride. And you have a place. Good dry barn?" I nod. "I can only give you food for a month. You'll have to take care of the rest. Come spring you can return him here or we can work out a price. I have a mare coming up from Tennessee next week so I'll have to know soon."

"Yes," I say before I can stop myself. "Yes, I'll take him, Mr. Fogg. I'll take him this weekend. He'll be just fine with me."

"Don't you want to think it over, honey?" Mr. Gowen asks, concerned. "Run it by a few people at home first?"

"No, Mr. Gowen. I think I can speak for my family and say we'd be pleased to take Sepia," for that's the name I have decided on.

Chapter 8

On my way to the barn tonight, I hear a formation of geese fly overhead. Each time a group passes, I look up or run to a window and stick my head out to hear their sound. It feels important to witness their flight south, respond in some way to the honking even if it is only to stare up at the V they make in the sky before disappearing over the pines. There is something sad to me about the honking of geese, though I know it is only their way of giving direction. What they say probably isn't sad at all and I only think it is because I don't understand their language.

I read a newspaper story once about a goose whose wing was injured as it flew through an ice storm. It went down in a marsh and three other geese landed with it, staying until the injured goose could fly again. The four geese found a fort made out of straw and sticks that some kids had made the summer before. They lived there for a week, keeping each other warm until a farmer found them and took them to his barn. In the spring they flew away in four different directions. The reporter who wrote the story speculated that they had probably had enough of each other, but I think they just knew when to let go.

Light filters down from the studio. Carmen must be in. I've stayed away from the barn since I overheard her argue with Grandmother. Tonight Suki sent me on a mission to go through Great-grandmother's trunk, which I've never opened before. I am looking for sequins. Suki told me there is a little bottle of sequins and beads near the top.

The trunk is too big to bring into the house, so it sits here covered in old tapestries and a thick layer of dust. Since there are no lights in this part of the barn, I wear Eva's headlamp. It's been a while since I've been here. Mr. Gowen has piled broken chairs in front of the trunk to make room for the hay. I push them out of the way, choose one with no legs to sit on on the floor. I blow dust off the brass latch, lift it up above my head. The scents of mildew and damp wood rise up into my nose. I never met Great-grandmother, but the sight of the linens she folded so carefully, the flowers pressed between glass, brings a tight feeling into my throat like sadness.

Suki said that in the far right corner underneath the pictures of Great-grandfather I will find the glass bottle of beads and sequins. I don't look for it right away. I pull out a yellowed newspaper clipping.

Harold Esmit Cooney Accepted to Academy of Inventors in Washington, D.C., Ceremony

A small, grainy photograph of Great-grandfather accompanies the headline. A tall, gaunt man with heavy, dark eyebrows wearing a gray suit and tweed cap. I look into his eyes, trying to find a resemblance to anyone I know. He is maybe a cross between Abraham Lincoln and Jimmy Stewart. I'm surprised the photograph isn't framed in gold and hung on the wall in the bathroom. I set the clipping, crisp with age, aside and try on a pair of long beige evening gloves, the kind ladies used to wear to a dance. They are a little tight. I pick up a box of old cufflinks, pins, buttons, clip-on rhinestone earrings. I open a small red velvet box containing a gold watch. As I lift out the watch, the lining of the box comes with it. Underneath, wedged into the corner, is a small piece of paper folded several times. I unfold it. Another newspaper clipping.

> Harold Esmit Cooney of County Road, Hawthorne, was arrested at his home Saturday evening as a result of a complaint

by Mrs. Esther Hodge, a neighbor of the Hansens. He was later released into the care of his wife, Isadora Cooney Hansen.

The rest of the clipping has been torn away. The date says February 25, 1943. The day Charlotte disappeared. I heard from Eva that when Harold found out Charlotte had disappeared during the storm, he started shouting her name into the wind and in his grief and his drunken state almost set the barn on fire. Harold was arrested for disturbing the peace. I fold up the paper and slip it back into the lining of the velvet box.

A jar of sequins and beads falls into my hand at that moment as if to say, "Here, that's enough. You don't have to look any further." I hear footsteps above my head. I put the bottle into my pocket and close the trunk. There are two sets of footsteps. I listen. Muffled voices. Not Grandmother. If it were Grandmother, I would know. Her deep voice stands out from the rest of my aunts' voices. I walk quickly and silently to the hay bales, climb up to the spot under the missing board, give it a shove, and turn off the headlamp. I can't believe I'm doing this after the last time, but old habits die hard. It's Mama. I can see the heel of her shoe on the floor.

"I can't stay long, Carmen. I have dinner in the oven," Mama says.

"Sit down, Maeve, please." Mama sits down.

Carmen's voice sounds tired, gentle. "Georgia's birthday is tomorrow, and after that I'll be going. I won't have another chance to speak to you before then, with all the preparations. Listen, Maeve. I know I can't change the way things are here. Believe me, I wish I could. But you all have the life you've chosen, and I'm grateful for all you've done with Georgia. She's a strong young woman. I'm not worried about her. She'll do fine. I'm worried about you." Her voice softens. "Who is going to fly with Georgia tomorrow? Eva? Suki?"

Silence.

"I'm not sure," Mama says weakly.

"Damn it, Maeve. When will you be sure? This is your chance to take back your power. You were the best flier in the family once, and now Mother has you convinced you're too frail. Are you? Too frail to fly with your own daughter on her birthday?"

"My daughter?" Mama asks.

"Yes. I can't do it, Maeve. You have to. Promise me you will fly with her."

I hear Mama shift around in her chair.

"It's not as easy as you think, Carmen. You don't know what it's like to live here."

"I think I do," Carmen says. "I think I can see it all very clearly."

"Mother is my only means of support. How could I have raised Georgia on my own? Taught her everything she needed to know? I don't have the luxury to rebel against Mother like you do. You have nothing to lose."

"I know. I've already lost it all."

Silence.

"Maeve, you have the power here. More than you know. If you could only see it. Take it. If you can't take it for yourself, take it for Georgia."

The barn door opens. Their words stop. I sink deep into the bales of hay. Silhouetted in the doorway stands Grandmother.

"Maeve!" she calls. Mama is silent. "Maeve, your pots are boiling over in the kitchen."

Grandmother's voice is high and irritated. She stands there for a moment and then the barn door swings closed. I breathe. There is a scraping of chairs above.

"Like she can't reach over and turn off the pots herself," Carmen says.

Mama gives a nervous laugh. "I have to go now," she says.

"Here, this is for you." Carmen turns and picks up a white envelope from the table and hands it to Mama. "There's a note inside explaining what it means. You'll want to share it with Eva and Suki." Carmen walks Mama to the door.

"I'm glad you came," Mama says, holding the envelope tentatively in her hands. "I've wanted you to see her for a long time."

"Thank you, Maeve. You've done a great job with her. Better than I would have done."

The door closes softly. I hear Mama's footsteps descend the stairs and cross the courtyard. Above me Carmen begins to cry. A mournful sound that seeps down through the floorboards and into the air of the barn. It's not like any crying I've ever heard before. It's a deep moaning that sends a rush of heat up into my belly, and I weep too. I feel like I've found something in this lonely sound that fills all the empty places of the barn. It is a deep wailing like the wind, like the sound of a goose falling out of the sky. Alone.

* * *

"Great. I knew they were there," Suki says, taking the little jar from my hand and holding it like precious contraband. She opens the lid and pours out a handful of glass beads mixed with silver sequins. "So pretty. Look, Georgia."

She holds them up to the light. They're beautiful, but I'm not thinking about beads at the moment. My mind is still back in the barn. No matter how hard I try to focus, my thoughts fly away. I watch Suki. *She's young,* I think. *So young.* She seems younger than I am. Her face is perfect. Soft skin and fine blond hair. She is like a picture of a Madonna I once saw in an art book in Eva's room. She threads a needle with her long, slender fingers and pulls its silver tip through one of the glass beads.

"These will finish the dress nicely. Did you have any trouble finding them?" Suki asks.

"No," I say. "They were right near the top."

"Good. You're brave, Georgia. I'm afraid to go into the barn at night. So many things you could trip over in the dark. And when the wind comes through . . ." She shivers. "I'm afraid of what I'll hear in there, you know?"

"I know," I say. "Sometimes it scares me, too."

Chapter 9

It is the morning of my birthday. I wake with the memory of a dream.

I am standing behind a pine tree in the clearing, dressed in animal skins. I carry a rattle in my hand. The moon in the sky is large and heavy, the color of butterscotch. I'm singing an old Abenaki song I learned from Grace, when a sound in the clearing interrupts me. Two women sit by a fire. One of the women is squatting and moaning. I can tell by the way she arches her back and holds on to the other woman's hand for balance that she is giving birth.

"You should have told me!" the birthing woman is saying over and over again. She cries as the other woman rises and begins to dance around the fire.

I look to my right, and a wolf sits on a stone next to me reading a newspaper. His coat is silver under the light of the moon.

"They should have told her, you know," the wolf says, putting down the paper. He raises his head and begins howling in unison with the woman in the clearing.

The woman who is dancing around the fire stops, and a group of geese on tall stilts continue dancing for her. One by one the geese lay eggs into the fire. The eggs pop open from the heat, blowing feathers up into the sky.

"They're really not helping her. Can you see that?" the wolf asks me. "They think they are, but they're not. What she needs is someone to tell her the truth. Don't you agree?"

I look up at the moon. It is rising and changing to a bright white. I would tell the woman the truth, *I think,* if I knew what the truth was.

I have what Grace refers to as dream hangover. A dream so clear and vivid that it lingers on into the morning and sometimes into the afternoon. Grace says the only cure for it is to write the dream down and open the window, take a few deep breaths, and shake your head back and forth until it clears. But this morning I just lie in the feeling of the dream and think about the night I was born.

Mama has never spoken to me of my birth. The only information I have has been passed down through Eva, who told me that on the night I came into the world there was a wild electrical storm that shut down power all over the state, an uncommon occurrence in northern Vermont in October. Eva and Grandmother delivered me by candlelight in the kitchen in front of the woodstove. That's all I know. I used to beg Mama to tell me about that night, but she never would.

"It was a true miracle how you came to us, Georgia," is all she would say.

Grace says it is possible to remember your own birth if you practice meditation or special yoga positions that will call forth the memory of your first breath, but the only thing I can recall when I close my eyes is a dim light and the sound of a woman weeping.

There is a birthday breakfast waiting for me in the kitchen. I can smell pancakes and Mama's special omelets. Alice is coming, and Mr. Gowen said he had to check the gutters so he'd stop in too. Mr. Gowen has made it for every one of my birthdays. He has never missed.

It is a sunny day and I am grateful. I can fly in bad weather, but I prefer it to be clear.

Before I go downstairs, I have to take a moment to consider Sepia. With all the preparations for today, he has been forgotten. My stomach jumps at the thought of actually having him here, but every time I try to imagine what I'll tell Grandmother, my mind goes blank. I'm planning to bring him over on Sunday afternoon while Grandmother is at Agnes Himpley's for tea. When she comes home, Sepia will already be settled in and there won't be anything she can do about it.

Actually there will be a lot she can do about it.

Mama told me a story about the time Suki brought home a dog she found wandering down the county road. Suki must have been eight at the time. It was a gentle black Lab that looked like it hadn't eaten in days. Grandmother had a fit, put the dog in the back of Beulah, and drove him to the pound in Hawthorne. There was no discussion about keeping him. I guess the only thing I have going for me is that Sepia will not fit in the back of Beulah.

I don't feel any different this morning. Sixteen feels exactly like fifteen, but when I walk into the kitchen Mama looks at me as if she is checking for signs.

"So, Georgia. How does it feel?"

I shrug. "Not any different. I don't have any gray hair, do I?" I say, bending over to show Mama the top of my head.

"No, none that I can see," Mama laughs. I study her face for a moment. She seems different this morning, brighter, larger. "Sit down, honey. Alice is going to be late, so we'll start without her." She calls my aunts and Grandmother in from the porch. "Georgia's here!" she says softly.

Eva comes in first, kisses me on the cheek. "Happy birthday, kid." She brings out a large package from behind her back. She has to hold it with both hands. "Hope you like it," she says.

I put it down on a bare space on the kitchen table and carefully pull back the paper. It is a watercolor of

Suki and me drinking lemonade in the meadow last summer. I remember when Eva did the sketch for it. It's beautiful. Eva's colors are bright and rich and swirled together so the whole thing looks good enough to eat.

"Thank you, Eva," I say, reaching over to hug her. "I love it! I didn't think you were going to do anything with that sketch."

"Well, I did," Eva says.

"One day when the art world is scanning the globe for original Eva Hansens, I will be one of the lucky owners," I say.

Eva laughs, walks over to the counter, and pours herself some juice. "See, Mother, I have one fan."

Grandmother smiles faintly. "You are very talented, Eva. I have always said that." Eva rolls her eyes.

Suki steps up next and holds out a small white box with a gold ribbon tied around it. "I have a song for you later too," she whispers. Inside her package is a pair of silver earrings with cobalt-blue stones. I can tell by their weight they are expensive. I look up at her. She smiles.

"I'll wear them tonight," I say.

I wonder how she could afford such a gift on her allowance. Grandmother must be thinking the same thing. "Exquisite, Suki," she says. I kiss Suki on the cheek.

Grandmother gives me her gift next. As always it

is a package of white handkerchiefs and a twenty-dollar gift certificate to the Book Corner in Garrison. "They have a good sale coming up this weekend," she adds. Out of the corner of my eye I see Suki and Eva exchange glances.

"Thank you, Grandmother." She steps back before I could possibly attempt to hug or kiss her. She does not care for public or private displays of affection.

"Okay, everyone. Sit down," Mama says. She brings a plate and lays it down in front of me. Buttermilk banana pancakes, tempeh bacon, and veggie sausages. On top of the stack of pancakes is a ring box, like a tiny house perched upon a cliff.

"Maeve, how sweet," says Suki.

I carefully pick up the box and open it. I know what it is before I look. Mama's opal ring. She had planned to wear it for her own solo once. I take it out and place it on my finger. Mama must have had it enlarged at the jeweler's, because it fits perfectly.

"It's not just for tonight. It's for you to keep."

"Thank you, Mama." I kiss her. A light kiss, barely grazing the soft skin of her cheek.

Mama serves pancakes and omelets to the rest of the group and sits down with a plate for herself. We say a blessing. We are not a religious family—I have never been to church in my life—but blessings are always said on special occasions. It is the one thing Mama insists upon.

"Thank you, Creator, for this clear day for flying.

Thank you for Georgia, for her health, beauty, and strength. Keep her safe in the sky. Amen."

The pancakes are delicious. They are not rice flour, but real mix pancakes. I look around the table at my aunts, Mama, and even Grandmother and I feel a clear moment of happiness.

There is a knock on the door and Alice pokes her head in. "Alice!" Mama says, standing up. "Come in. Here, sit next to Georgia."

Alice is dressed up for my birthday in black silk pants and a long India print shirt under a gold vest.

Mama serves Alice a large stack of pancakes and a glass of orange juice. *We seem like such a normal family today,* I think.

"How is your mother, Alice?" Grandmother asks. Grace is a person Grandmother would never speak to on the street and yet she is always interested in knowing what Grace is doing and how she is.

"Oh, fine, Mrs. Hansen. She delivered four babies last week."

"Were they all okay?" asks Mama.

"Oh, yeah," says Alice, sipping her juice. "All Grace's babies come out fine. One was a breech, but Grace has delivered at least fifteen breeches. A piece of cake."

I think, *A piece of cake for Grace, but maybe not for the mother.*

"Your mother is a very capable woman," says Grandmother. End of conversation.

There is a long silence. Everyone eats. Suki is the first to push her plate away and pat her stomach. "Any more and I'll explode." Suki does not have much capacity. "I have to make a couple of tucks in Georgia's dress," she says. "Do you want to see it, Alice?"

"Sure," Alice says. "Just let me finish this stack." Alice knows about my initiation ceremony. She thinks it's a nice ritual, being welcomed as a woman into the family, but she has no idea about the flying.

Before Suki and Alice can leave, there is another knock on the door and Carmen lets herself in. The mood in the room changes. Grandmother stiffens. Mama looks down at her plate. Alice looks at me. Carmen is wearing a bright red shirt with ballooning purple pants. Her black hair falls straight down her back. I feel a rush of pride and it surprises me.

"Alice, this is my . . . aunt Carmen. Carmen, this is my friend Alice St. Clair. She lives down the road."

Carmen smiles at Alice. "I knew your mother a long time ago," she says. "She is a good midwife."

Alice looks surprised. "I didn't know you had *another* aunt." She says it like I have dozens of them growing on trees in the backyard and pick a new one anytime I wish.

I just nod. "Carmen lives in California," I say. "She doesn't come very often."

"She's leaving tomorrow," Grandmother adds, giving me a sharp look.

"That's right," Carmen says. "I'll be flying out early tomorrow. I came for Georgia's birthday." It always amazes me how well my aunts cover up the true facts of our life.

"Oh," says Alice. "I hate to fly. It always seems so strange to me, being up inside a long metal tube eating lasagna thirty thousand feet above the earth watching a movie on a little screen that rolls down out of the ceiling. My uncle Raymond was in a plane once that lost one of its engines and one wheel on takeoff. The pilot managed a water landing and everyone got out. It was a miracle. My uncle never flew after that."

Everyone stares at Alice. None of us has ever flown in an airplane, of course, so this sounds terrifying.

"Don't worry, Alice," Carmen says. "I'll be safe. I've flown this particular airline all my life. I have complete confidence." She helps herself to a plate of pancakes and stands leaning against the counter. It is so apparent to me how alone Carmen is. How used to being alone she has become. I stand up.

"You can have my seat," I say to her. "Alice and I are going upstairs to look at my dress."

Carmen smiles at me. "Thank you, Georgia. I have something for you first." She puts down her plate and pulls a white envelope from the pocket of her purple balloon pants.

Grandmother stands up. "I would like to speak with you both in the study," she says.

"No, Mother. If you wish to say anything, you may say it now. Let's stop the private conversations. Open it, Georgia," Carmen says. I can feel Alice looking at all of us.

"No," says Grandmother.

I look up. Someone is standing in the doorway. Mr. Gowen.

"Georgia Brown. I just stopped to give my birthday wishes to you." He smiles his gap-toothed smile. "Myra," he says, tipping his hat to Grandmother. "I have a little something for Georgia. Outside." He gestures with his head in the direction of the kitchen window. I'm surprised to see a dark green horse trailer parked behind his red pickup. This isn't going according to plan. "Maybe this isn't a good time," he says, looking at Carmen and then at Grandmother. "I can come back later."

"Come in, Mr. Gowen," Carmen says. "We're just finishing our conversation here."

Grandmother strikes her fist against the table, making the silverware dance. "I will not have the entire town of Hawthorne knowing my private affairs."

"Mr. Gowen and Alice are not the entire town of Hawthorne," says Carmen. "They're friends. Open it, Georgia."

I look up at all of them. No one is breathing. They are all waiting for me. "I know what this is, Grandmother." I look at Carmen. "I know because I've been listening in on your conversations through the floor of the studio." My heart is racing. "I know it's a piece of land Great-grandmother Isadora left to Carmen and that she wants to give me because . . ." I look at Carmen and then at Mama and they both look back, waiting. "Because she wants me to have it and I want to use it for . . . my horse." I might as well spill it right now. "Mr. Gowen has delivered my birthday present today. I did not ask your permission, Grandmother. I have asked all my life and my requests have always been denied. I will take care of the horse by myself on my own land." Grandmother rises from the table, glares at me, and storms out of the kitchen. Carmen smiles. I fold the deed into the pocket of my overalls and walk outside with Mr. Gowen.

Sepia is standing patiently in the trailer. Mr. Gowen and I open the door and back him out. He seems taller out in the open. "Oh, thank you," I say, throwing my arms around Mr. Gowen's neck. "Thank you."

Mr. Gowen turns a little pink and laughs. "No problem, Georgia Brown."

"How come you brought Sepia today, Mr. Gowen? I thought he was coming on Sunday."

"Well, Fogg's new mare came earlier than expected and that man had ants up his pants over getting Sepia out of there, so I thought I'd surprise you."

"You did," I say.

Carmen comes up beside me. I look at her. I take

her in for the first time. Her hair, eyes, hands, and the smell of her. Spice and incense, and I want to say, "Who are you, really?" but the words never reach my lips.

"Well, quite a display of honesty in there, Georgia." Her eyes are laughing at me. "I hope you have the courage to tell the whole story sometime." Fear gathers in the bottom of my stomach. Fear and then anger. It amazes me how easily Carmen can push me to anger. I narrow my eyes at her and turn to pat Sepia's neck.

"Mr. Gowen," Carmen says.

"Carmen," says Mr. Gowen. "How are you, honey?" He wraps her in a long hug. "I heard from Maeve you were back in town. I been meaning to stop by."

"I was hoping you would," Carmen says.

I am surprised they would even know each other, but it seems they do. Very well, in fact.

"It's been a long time," says Mr. Gowen. Carmen nods.

"I see you've been taking good care of Georgia, like you promised," Carmen says, wiping at her eyes.

Mr. Gowen smiles. "Ain't always been so easy around here, but we sure do try." He gives me a wink.

"Are you going to take him out?" asks Carmen.

"Oh, can I, Mr. Gowen? Can I take him for a short ride?"

"No, honey, this horse has got to be fed now. If you're sure he can stay."

"He can stay," I say. I am aware of a crowd on the back porch, but there is no sign of Grandmother. "I thought I'd set up a little place in the barn for now."

Suki and Eva come over and stand next to me. "Whoa, Georgia. Brave girl," says Eva.

"What do you think Mother will do now?" asks Suki in a whisper.

"Nothing," says Carmen. "If you all stand by each other, there is nothing she can do." Carmen pulls out two white envelopes and hands one to Suki and one to Eva. "These are for you," she says. "It is a copy of Isadora's will. I always suspected Isadora left us each something. It took my lawyer the last six months to piece everything together. Maeve was given the house, I was given the studio and barn, complete with spy hole"—she gives me a half smile—"and twelve acres on the east hill. You were each given ten acres and fifty thousand dollars. You just have to claim it." Suki and Eva stare at Carmen as if she is speaking another language. "All Mother really owns is the land the cemetery is on and seven acres surrounding the clearing."

Alice walks over. I'd forgotten completely about her. "You certainly have an interesting family," she says, not the least upset about any of it. "Wish I could stay all day. I hate to miss any more excitement, but

Grace is waiting for me. I have to get to school." I give her a hug.

"I'll see you Saturday night," I tell her.

"Okay," she says, opening up her backpack and removing a small, flat package. "This is for you, Georgia. It's from Grace and me."

"Thanks," I say, opening the wrapping. It's a dream-catcher. Three circles of woven branches and in the center a turkey feather and six beads. A little note attached. "To our Georgia. May you catch all your dreams."

Chapter 10

My family will form the circle at dusk in the clearing. I have an hour before I need to prepare myself, so I climb up the east hill to the cemetery. It will be a good evening for flying; the sky is clear and pink at the horizon, only a few clouds.

I've come up here looking for answers. I'm no longer afraid Carmen will tell Grandmother. I'm afraid I will.

I sit down beside Louisa, pick a few dried leaves away from her stone, and wrap my sweater tightly around me. A field mouse scurries away into the woods with a nut in its mouth. I wish I were that little mouse tonight with nothing else on my mind but eating my nut for dinner and curling up in a hole. Instead I have to prepare for Grandmother's question. Do I lie to stay in a family in which I'm not even sure I belong, or do I speak the truth and be sent away? I can't decide. I'm tired. I'm afraid. I can't ask Mama or Suki or Eva to help me. I can't ask Carmen. I can only ask the women who came before.

Louisa's stone is in the best condition. Surrounded by the others, it has not taken the beating of wind and snow and rain as the others have.

LOUISA CARMELINA STRAVONA HANSEN
1862–1924
BELOVED MOTHER OF
GILDA MEREDITH FRANKLIN HANSEN

I wonder what mine will say one day. "Beloved and obedient daughter"? "Keeper of Secrets"? I wonder if Louisa had any idea it would come to this. If the first time she flew out over the Atlantic Ocean, she had any inkling that all her female descendants would have to carry the burden of her action.

"So, Louisa? What should I do tonight?" I know she isn't anywhere below me, so I look up and address the sky in case she's cruising overhead. I want a sign. A hawk circling twice if I should tell the truth. A snowstorm if I should lie. The wind blows past my ears. Nothing.

"Any of you, then?" I say, speaking to Gilda, Charlotte, Isadora, Harold. "Do you have anything worthwhile to contribute on this matter?"

I want to be free of Grandmother's rules, but at what price? I begin to cry. "Please," I whisper. "Help me. I don't know what to do."

There is no answer, no sign of a hawk, no change in the weather. Just the knowing silence of the dead.

* * *

Suki has laid my dress out on the bed with silk stockings and a pair of black flats with a strap across the top. Mama wove a garland of fresh flowers for my headpiece.

I sit in the big overstuffed chair in my room, staring at my dress, a candle lit beside me on the nightstand. In the candlelight the beads sparkle. A magic dress.

I fold my jeans neatly over the back of the chair and take off my shirt. I blow on my hands, which are cold from sitting in the cemetery too long. I'm still hoping for a sign, a word, something so I will know what to say when the time comes, but I fear no help will arrive.

I slip on a silk chemise with a long slit up to the top of the thigh. I dot the back of my ears with a drop of Eva's Paris Passion she left on my bureau. I'm wearing it for good luck. I kneel down by the side of the bed and close my eyes, let my hands fan out over the silk and beads. Suki finished the neckline and hem. It must have taken her all day. My fingers come to a bump in the fabric and I open my eyes and reach up inside the dress, turning it inside out. Suki has sewn a small pocket into the seam with a little button clasp. I unbutton it, lift the flap of material, pull out a folded slip of paper. I open it on the quilt. The light is dim, so I bring it to the candle on the nightstand. It is written in Suki's precise hand.

Be like the bird
That, pausing in her flight
Awhile on boughs too slight,
Feels them give way
Beneath her and sings,
Knowing that she hath wings.

—VICTOR HUGO

Suki's favorite quote. I smile, fold it back up, and button it into the small pocket. I carefully slip the dress over my head, its silky blackness enveloping me. I tie the silk sash around my waist, admiring my own fine stitching of the tiny rust-colored horse. Next I brush out my hair. I will let it hang loose tonight. I pin in the garland, apply some lipstick Mama gave me, put on my shoes, take in my full reflection in the mirror. Perfect. I blow out the candle and walk downstairs.

Mama is waiting for me in the kitchen along with Eva and Suki. Carmen comes in the back door. Even Grandmother is there in the corner, sipping tea. She is in charge of rituals. No matter how angry she is, she has to show up. Mama smiles at me. She hands out the lanterns and we go outside. It is chilly, but we do not wear coats. The bonfire will keep us warm.

I stop for a minute in the barn to check on Sepia, who seems happy. Mr. Gowen and I stacked hay bales in a large square for a temporary stall. I pat him on the neck. I would miss Sepia and Mr. Gowen. I'm not sure if I could think about never seeing them again.

In silence we walk up to the clearing. My feet feel heavy. My heart is racing. There is some light in the sky when we leave the barn, but by the time we reach the clearing, it is dark. Eva has been collecting brush all week long. Branches and logs are stacked high in the center of the circle marked with large round stones. There should be enough brush to last until dawn. It will help me if there are a few embers still burning, so I can see where I'm landing. Eva strikes a match to balls of newspaper stuck in at the bottom of the pile. It smokes at first and then begins to burn. We stand around it. Six women evenly spaced.

Grandmother's voice breaks the silence and I jump at the sound of my name.

"Georgia Louisa Hansen, have you come to fly?"

"Yes," I answer. My voice cracks.

"Are you prepared to join the family of fliers?"

"Yes," I say.

She turns to Eva. "Eva Meredith Hansen, is this woman prepared to complete her solo flight on this night?"

"Yes," answers Eva.

"Georgia Louisa Hansen, have you respected your teacher?"

"I have."

"Have you followed her instructions while in the air?"

"I have."

"Have you waited until this night to fly unattended in the sky?"

I pause and look around the circle. While she waits for my reply, Grandmother reaches over and adjusts the collar on Mama's dress, giving her a disapproving look. Mama shrinks from her touch, and I can see how her whole body pulls itself in and becomes smaller. A tiny gesture. A subtle turning away and inward. It's probably been happening for years and I never saw it before now. But something about it makes everything clear to me.

I scan the faces illuminated by the fire. Six women including myself. Five lives ruled by one. Even Carmen, standing tall and proud beside me. Whatever it was that she did once was not worth Grandmother's wrath. I know it wasn't. Louisa Hansen never intended our gift of flight to be a burden. We were not meant to give away our power. We were not meant to live in fear. Anger begins to rise inside me. Anger at how wrong this all is. Suddenly it no longer matters what will happen. I know what I need to do. For myself, for Mama, for all of us.

"No, Grandmother." My voice is clear and strong. "I have flown on one occasion alone, without supervision."

Mama turns and looks at me. Her eyes are wide. Grandmother glares over the climbing flames.

"In the daylight," I add. I can hear Suki and Eva suck in their breath at the same time. Carmen smiles.

There is a long silence. The fire crackles. One wet log hisses and spits.

"Then there will be no initiation here tonight," Grandmother says, standing firmly on the ground like a stone. "We will discuss the repercussions of your actions back at the house. You know the rules." She bends and begins to collect her things.

"No!" I look around the circle. "No!" It's Mama.

"Maeve!" Grandmother's voice is strained. "Remember your place."

"Where is my place, Mother? In the kitchen? Washing dishes? I have raised Georgia all these years, encouraged her, loved her, while you stood back and judged, found fault, made me think I was small. Now you ask me to stand by and watch you rob her of her birthright. I will not." Mama pauses. Her legs are shaking. "I've lied to Georgia since she was little. I raised my sister's child as if she were my own. I have lived in fear of the truth, in fear of my own life, in fear of you, Mother."

I look at Mama and then across the circle at Carmen and that gnawing sensation in my belly that has been there since the night I first saw Carmen begins to dissolve. I put the puzzle together in my mind, and suddenly that missing piece is no longer missing. I don't know what to feel. Angry, hurt, confused. I feel them all, but more than these I feel relief, as if I haven't taken a breath of fresh air in days and now I can. Sweet, cool air. Everyone's eyes are on me. Even Grandmother waits for my reaction. I stare silently at Mama. I can think of nothing to say.

For a long time no one speaks. The fire shoots up high and we all back away from the heat.

"We will take a vote," says Carmen. "All in favor of Georgia being initiated tonight say 'Yes.' "

Everyone's voice rises in a powerful "Yes." All except Grandmother's.

Carmen speaks again. "We've all made mistakes, Mother. We've kept the truth from one another. It's time to change the rules. We can make new ones. Rules we can live with."

Grandmother holds up her hand. "Enough! I can see for myself how things are. I do not need a sermon, especially from you." Her voice is hard. "If you initiate Georgia tonight, that is your business. I will have no part in it. The tradition means something to me, though I can see it means nothing to you." She picks up her lantern and heads for the house.

Grandmother is stubborn, and she rarely stays around to argue. She feels it is beneath her to enter into debate with any of her daughters. She is used to having her own way on most matters and threatening us with banishment if we challenge her. With Carmen's news about Isadora's will, she has nothing to hold over us any longer, and I think she knows it.

There is a moment of silence as we watch Grandmother's dark figure disappear into the trees.

"She'll come around," says Suki.

"Or she won't," Eva adds quietly. "But even if she doesn't, we have each other."

For the first time since she came, Carmen is included in the "we." Suki pulls her mandolin from its case and begins the song she wrote for tonight. It is about flying home at dawn. She teaches us the refrain and we join her. Five women's voices rising up above the pines.

When the fire is at its height, each woman steps forward and offers me one blessing. Eva brings my bundle. "May you have a home on the earth and in the sky." She straps it around me.

Suki hands me a box of matches. "For warmth on the journey."

Carmen comes up and I look into her eyes. My eyes, my nose, my face. Why didn't I see it before?

She removes the garland of flowers from my head and replaces it with a soft wool hat. "May your ears not freeze to the sides of your head." Everyone laughs, and somehow the tension of Grandmother's presence finally leaves the circle.

Mama is last. She gives me her thick black sweater and her hand. "I'll be flying with you to the ridge," she says. I nod. I am too stunned to speak.

Before we take off, Mama turns to Eva. "Thank you, Eva," Mama says.

"My pleasure. Georgia was an excellent student." Eva kisses Mama on the cheek. "I'm glad for you, Maeve. You should have been flying with her all along."

Then Eva turns to me. "Well, kid, it's been fun. This is your big moment. Fly like the wind!"

I hug Eva and give Mama my hand. She seems younger, a great weight taken from her shoulders. The wind picks up, we start running together, and suddenly it doesn't matter to me about Sepia or Carmen or Grandmother. I am holding the hand of a woman who has loved me all my life.

Chapter 11

Together we fly to the ridge. Mama holds my hand the whole way. We're both nervous. She is a bit shaky and occasionally glances over to make sure I'm still beside her and know where I am going. Sixteen years of being grounded can work on a person's confidence, but she does just fine. She is beaming, and I know she is proud of herself for speaking up to Grandmother and coming with me. We both land about a hundred feet from the edge. Behind us, the house is dark except for a light in Grandmother's window. I feel sorry for her sitting all alone with her rules and traditions. I wonder what she could be doing. Certainly not reading. When she is upset, she is unable to concentrate. The only thing that has ever calmed her is flying, but I don't think she would go out tonight. There is a chance she could bump into me, and I don't think she'd want that. I see the shaft of light peeking out from under the barn door. I have a strong urge to check on Sepia. Mama reads my mind. "I'll check on him before I go to bed," she assures me.

Mama spreads a blanket on the ground and we sit down in our beautiful black dresses. It's chilly, so I wrap myself in the sweater Mama gave me. She does not look cold at all. She does not look small or frail or weak. She looks strong and determined.

"When Carmen was eighteen years old," Mama begins, "she met a boy at the Valentine's Day dance over at the Garrison Grange. Mother had forbidden Carmen to go. But Carmen was always wild like the wind, taking chances. Sam was nineteen, shy, handsome. He was a student at the university home for the weekend. After the dance, Carmen and Sam spent the night together in a little sugar shack on his father's farm. When Carmen returned home before dawn, she told Mother she had been flying as usual. Sam came home every weekend after that and Carmen would meet him.

"After a couple of months, Carmen started getting sick in the mornings and she knew she was pregnant. When she couldn't hide it any longer, Carmen told Mother that she was going to marry Sam, and Mother was furious. Not that Carmen was pregnant, but that she wanted to bring a man into the family. Mother could tolerate a baby, but she could not risk having a man who would challenge her authority, especially a bright man like Sam.

"It was hard on all of us. Mother forbade Carmen to tell Sam or ever to see him again. The pregnancy was hard on Carmen. It took all her strength to carry you. She wasn't strong enough to stand up to Mother then, so she spent most evenings in her room plotting to run away with you and Sam after you were born. Eva and Suki were little then, ten and eight, but I was fifteen and I knew what was going on. Sometimes I would bump into Sam in town and he would ask me about Carmen. I'd tell him she was fine but that she was not allowed to see him. He had no idea about you being on the way then. He only found out later.

"You came early. We had planned to take Carmen to the university medical center when the time came, but there was no time. Grace was a friend of mine. She was only twenty-three but she knew about delivering babies from her old Abenaki granny up in St. Albans. It's true that you were born during an electrical storm. The power and phone lines were down that night, Mother was out with Beulah, so I ran down to Grace's house and begged her to come. She didn't want to do it at first. Alice was not even a year old then, and Grace had never delivered a baby alone. But there was no one else, and Carmen needed someone who knew more than I did, so Grace finally agreed to come.

"Alice slept in my bed while Grace delivered you in the kitchen in front of the woodstove. It was a cold night, and the stove was the best source of heat in the house. We lit candles all over the kitchen so when you came out it was like a church in there.

"Carmen hardly made any noise at all. It was almost like she left her body entirely during the birth. When she saw you for the first time, she began weeping. 'She'll never let me keep her,' she said over and over again. 'She'll never let me keep her.'

"Well, somehow Sam had heard about Carmen being pregnant. It was amazing that anyone found out, given the way your grandmother covered over the whole thing. Carmen had graduated from Hawthorne Valley the spring before, so your grandmother told everyone she was off at a fancy college in Rhode Island and she wouldn't be home until Christmas. I don't know what she intended to tell people when Carmen appeared with a baby in her arms at the Hawthorne post office. It never came to that, though. Maybe Mother knew it never would." Mama looks down at her hands.

"The morning after you were born, Sam drove over. I think Grace probably told him what had happened. He wrapped you and Carmen up in thick wool horse blankets and put you both inside the cab of his truck. They say everything in life is timing, and in this case it was true. Mother pulled into the driveway as Sam was leaving. There was a bad scene.

Mother told the two of them they could go and never come back as far as she was concerned, but the baby had to stay here. If you had been a boy, Carmen could have taken you, but you were a flier. Mother would never let you go.

"I think Carmen knew all along she was totally unprepared to be a parent. Mother convinced her she could never care for a baby with only Sam to help. Carmen was so weak then . . . she just gave in. Mother paid them a lot of money to start a life somewhere else with the agreement that Carmen would leave you here and not try to see you until the eve of your sixteenth birthday. It's strange that Mother even made that concession, but she did.

"Carmen and Sam agreed to leave and try to make a life for themselves in California, where Sam had a cousin who lived by the ocean. I remember the way Carmen looked at me that morning as she handed you to me. She said, 'Take care of my baby, Maeve, will you? Take good care of her.' I nodded and tried to smile, but I was crying too hard as we hugged each other. She had to go, I knew that. But it hurt all the same. Her leaving without you seemed cruel and unfair, and that was just the beginning of her grief. Sam was killed in a car accident a year after they moved out there. Carmen sent a note to tell us. I thought Mother would have pity and invite Carmen home once Sam was gone, but Mother would not even let us respond to Carmen's letter.

"Mother helped care for you while I finished school, and then when I graduated I took over full-time. Thinking back, I see that it was a perfect plan for her. I was shy and quiet. Mother had successfully convinced me that I was frail and dependent on her for my living, so I was easy to control. She gave you to me because she knew I wouldn't try to leave.

"I wrote to Carmen once a month telling her all about you, but Carmen said it was too painful to hear about you long distance, especially without Sam. She asked me to stop.

"I believe neither Sam nor Carmen ever wanted to leave you. All I can say is that we were young and afraid and Mother controlled our lives so rigidly we could barely think for ourselves. You broke that for all of us, Georgia, and I am grateful."

She stops and we look at each other. I don't know what to say.

"I have always felt bad about not telling you the story before. I meant to, but by the time I'd worked up the courage, you'd stopped asking. I think of you as my daughter, Georgia, but you are Carmen's daughter too. And in her way, Carmen loves you very much. She has spent her life alone. She lost you and Sam and her entire family before she turned twenty. Banished for the simple act of loving another human being. That's all, Georgia. That's the story. You were born into this family of fliers, and now it is your time to fly." She kisses my forehead. She smells like lavender and woodsmoke.

I nod, take off my shoes in a kind of trance, tighten the bundle around my waist, and adjust my wool hat. I stand up, stretch. I wish I could say something to Mama, but nothing comes to me. All the questions that should be in my mind are not there. I feel like someone has stuffed my brain full of cotton and I can no longer put words together to speak. Instead I give Mama a little wave, touch my finger to the horse on my sash for luck, and begin running like I did the day Carmen made me so angry. The day I knew she would never leave without turning my life upside down.

* * *

It's strange at first having no one beside me, and not as beautiful as the daylight. Only black ahead. But there are a half moon and stars.

I have to focus on where I am going. I have to remember what Eva taught me about clearing my mind. I listen to my breath and stay awake to the surroundings, let thoughts pass through my mind like clouds. *Pine tree. Breathe. Wind out of the east. Breathe. Mama. Breathe. Carmen. Breathe. Breathe. Breathe.* I head north, keeping a hundred feet above the tree line. It takes me about ten minutes to reach the river. I circle a few times and then fly over the pine forest at the edge of the reserve. Luckily there is some light from the moon and I can see the reflection of water off the small lake Eva pointed out to me the night before last. I make preparations to land.

As I descend, noise behind me like a bunch of chattering women breaks my reverie. Geese! Looking for a place to land for the night. I quickly increase my altitude. Geese are incredibly strong in formation. A flock could knock me out of the sky. The direction of their honking changes and I can tell they are below me now, passing underneath. I am relieved. Now they won't fly into me—and they won't poop on me. I can't imagine how hard it would be to get goose poop out of my hair.

I look below me and the sky has turned white. Snow geese! The tops of their sleek bodies like angels against the blackness. Like clouds. For a moment I imagine I can land on top of them and they will carry me off to some enchanted kingdom on the other side of the sun, like Thumbelina riding to the land of the flower fairies on the back of a swallow. For several minutes we fly on parallel planes. I am thrilled to be one of them. They honk and I honk back, though I'm not a strong honker myself. Soon, though, they move on in search of their own camp for the night. "Good night. Safe landing," I call out, hoping they can understand me.

I have a strong desire to turn to my right and ask Eva for advice. But I am on my own. This is the most difficult part of flying for me, judging the distance and timing on descent. I find that clear patch again by the lake and land, gently pressing my arms back and closer and closer to my sides. I land running, bringing my arms forward and stopping right at the edge of the lake. I take a deep breath. The woods are quiet, no sign of my geese friends.

I shake out my arms. I was tense on the flight and now I ache from holding my body stiff against the wind. Exhausted from the day, all I want is to find a sheltered place inside a stand of pine, open my bundle, and fall asleep. It takes me several minutes to find the right spot and unstrap the bundle from around my waist. Inside, Mama has rolled up a pair of heavy sweatpants and a thick flannel jacket, one extra pair of socks, and a chocolate bar. I put everything on, tucking my dress into my pants, and wriggle into my sleeping bag.

The woods are quiet at this time of the year. Only the sound of a few stubborn beech leaves scratching against one another in the breeze. There are no crickets to sing me to sleep. Too cold for crickets. I imagine if I were not comfortable being out in the night this might frighten me, but I find it strangely soothing. As I lie on the ground, all the events of the day drain out into the earth beneath me. I decide I have my whole life to figure everything out. For now I must sleep.

In the early hours of the morning I am awakened

by the crack of a branch near my head. I open my eyes. I do not move. The sky is still black.

"Georgia?" a voice whispers. A chill goes up my spine. It is very eerie to hear your name whispered in the woods when you think you are alone.

"Are you awake?" Maybe it's a dream. Maybe it's an old Abenaki spirit come to haunt me. After yesterday I wouldn't be surprised at anything.

I nod so as not to offend any spirit, dream or otherwise. Carmen's face bends down over me. I breathe a sigh. "Carmen!" I sit up.

"You snore," she says, laughing.

"If you'd had a day like I had yesterday, you'd snore too."

Carmen laughs again, sits down cross-legged on the ground beside me. She has changed out of her dress and is wearing a thick pair of black wool pants and a sweater. There is an uncomfortable silence.

"I'm on my way home. I didn't say goodbye to you or give you this." She hands me a locket. "On one side is a picture of me when I was about your age. On the other side is a picture of your father. Samuel Gowen."

"Gowen?"

"Yes, Sam was Mr. Gowen's oldest boy." Her lips turn down a little at the mention of his name.

"So Mr. Gowen is my . . . grandfather?" I ask.

"That's right. Sam made Mother promise that Mr. Gowen could see you whenever he wished. I made

Mr. Gowen promise he'd look out for you, not let the old lady get too tight a grip around your soul. And Mr. Gowen told Mother that if she ever tried to keep him from seeing you, he'd tell you everything one day. So Grandmother hired Mr. Gowen to work for us and in exchange he promised not to tell."

"Geez, Carmen. I'll never get back to sleep now. I don't think my brain can handle any more new information."

"I know, it's a lot. But I won't see you for a while and I wanted you to have this."

"Thanks," I say, taking the locket. I open it. My parents. I stare at their faces for a long time, trying to see myself. The man on the right-hand side is tan and looks like Mr. Gowen. I can see something of myself there too, in the eyes. Carmen is beautiful. Her hair even longer and her cheeks fuller.

"I know you're my real mother, but Mama feels like my mother," I say.

"She is. More than I am. I gave birth to you, but I would never bind you to me. I'm not the mother type. You know? Stick with Maeve on that one, okay?"

"Okay."

"I don't want anything from you, Georgia. I just wanted to make sure you knew the truth. Everyone has the right to know the truth. And I wanted to make sure you weren't living in fear. But I can see that's something you'd never choose. I'm proud to know you, Georgia Louisa Hansen. Come visit me, if you like. Maeve can tell you where to find me. I have to get going now. I have a life to get back to, believe it or not."

I nod. "Have a safe trip," I say. I want to give Carmen something to take back with her, but all I can think of is a piece of advice. "Eva says it's best to avoid going over the Great Lakes."

"I go that way on purpose." Carmen smiles at me. "I like a good strong wind. It gives me something to come up against."

I stretch out my hand. Carmen takes it and pulls me to her in a fierce hug. Brief and hard so when we pull away I can still feel the imprint of her body against mine. She runs the tips of her fingers over the crown of my head and disappears into the trees.

⋆ ⋆ ⋆

They say it is always darkest before the dawn. It's true. The sky is the deep black of obsidian. Dawn seems far away, but it is very close. I roll up my bundle, slip the locket over my neck, and tuck it inside my dress. There is no cliff to run off here. There is only a small hill on the other side of the lake. I'm not as confident with this kind of takeoff, but I remember Eva's words. "It's easier with a cliff, but you can take off from the bottom of a dry riverbed if necessary."

When I reach the hill I pull my hat tighter over my

ears and run up as fast as I can. By the time I reach the top, I have enough air beneath me to let go and fly.

There is a faint hint of light at the horizon as I come into view of the house. No lights are on. The widow's walk looks deserted and lonely. Before I head for the clearing there is something I need to do. I fly over the roof of the barn in the direction of the upper meadow and hover for a moment above the cemetery. In all the years I've flown with Eva, we've never once come up here. This is my first time viewing it from the air and I laugh, thinking this must be what Louisa and Gilda see whenever they pass over. The stones look smaller from this angle and not as crooked as teeth. More like little gray fingers reaching up out of the darkness.

"Thank you," I call down to the stones. "Thank you for the gift of flight." A meadowlark whistles in the dogwood trees, a leaf brushes my cheek. I roll over once and fly east in the direction of the dawn, toward the fading embers of the fire and the dark figures of three women waiting.

ABOUT THE AUTHOR

RITA MURPHY lives in Vermont with her husband and son. She dances and writes stories in a little red barn in the country where the nights are clear and the wind is just right for flying. This is her first novel, and she is at work on her next.